MALAFORMED
REALITIES

VOLUME SEVEN

THOMAS M. MALAFARINA

**HELLBENDER
BOOKS**

an imprint of Sunbury Press, Inc.
Mechanicsburg, PA USA

an imprint of Sunbury Press, Inc.
Mechanicsburg, PA USA

For information about special discounts for bulk purchases, please contact Sunbury Press Orders Dept. at (855) 338-8359 or orders@sunburypress.com.

To request one of our authors for speaking engagements or book signings, please contact Sunbury Press Publicity Dept. at publicity@sunburypress.com.

FIRST HELLBENDER BOOKS EDITION: June 2024

Set in Adobe Garamond Pro | Interior design by Crystal Devine | Cover design by Lawrence Knorr | Edited by Lawrence Knorr

Publisher's Cataloging-in-Publication Data
Names: Malafarina, Thomas M., author.
Title: Malaformed realities / Thomas M. Malafarina.
Description: First trade paperback edition. | Mechanicsburg, PA : Hellbender Books, 2024.
Summary: Thomas Malafarina strikes again with 18 spine-tingling tales of horror.
Identifiers: ISBN 979-8-88819-197-2 (softcover).
Subjects: FICTION / Horror | FICTION / Short Stories (single author).

Designed in the USA
0 1 1 2 3 5 8 13 21 34 55

For the Love of Books!

For my amazing and beautiful wife, JoAnne.
The greatest gift a man could ask for is to have
an incredible woman with whom to share his life.
Somehow, without ever asking or daring to hope,
I have been blessed with such a gift.

CONTENTS

INTRODUCTION

Here we are with the seventh volume of my short story collection, Malaformed Realities. Then again, with over 200 short stories to date and six previous volumes, this should not come as any great surprise to anyone. My invisible muses have been quite busy bombarding me with story ideas, and as a devoted scribe and supplicant, I have been doing my part to appease them and put these stories down on paper.

Does it mean I have lost interest in writing novels? Nope, not even a little. It's just that some stories start small and stay small. Others start small and evolve into something more extensive, like a long short story or a novella. If my muses determine, others may become novels, and others might be a series of books. I have no idea; I'm just the guy with the keyboard who puts these inspirations down for you to read.

So here is *Malaformed Realities Volume 7*. It's got some sci-fi, some mystery, and lots of horror. This collection focuses slightly more on death, despair, and disease than most. That's likely because I wrote many of these stories during the COVID-19 pandemic. Please forgive my dark mood during those most troubling times. I'm sure you all can relate. That being said, I hope you enjoy this latest collection, and for the record, by the time you read this, I will be well into *Volume 8*, maybe *Volume 9*, and even possibly *Volume 10*. It all depends upon powers more remarkable than my own.

THOMAS M. MALAFARINA
June 2024

BLOODY CREEK

The black Nissan Quest sat idling along the highway, its driver leaning out the open window and feeling the cool autumn breeze gently moving the hairs on his arms, simultaneously raising goosebumps. At least he assumed the goosebumps were the result of the draft and not from his unease. He was staring at the worn and faded wooden road sign, which hung noticeably askew. It was one of those signs with a point sawed into the end for directional purposes. It bore the name Bloody Creek.

The weathered appearance of the thing made it seem both eerie as well as foreboding as if the name of the place alone wasn't creepy enough to raise gooseflesh. He realized he was not only looking at a piece of local history but, in essence, a piece of his history. The sign pointed to a small plot of land, which had gotten its name from a massacre occurring there centuries earlier.

According to local historians, back in the mid seventeen hundreds, the area had been known as Blaudie's Creek, named after the local farmer Clayton Jackson Blaudie, who owned the land adjacent to the small creek. Blaudie had been an early settler in the area. He and his family lived in a tiny one-room cabin Blaudie had built himself. Farming his land and hunting in the surrounding forest provided the Blaudie family with sufficient food and clothing to survive during the cold winter months.

Things had been going well until tragedy hit one fall evening when Blaudie, his wife, Emily, and three of their children were brutally slaughtered. Their scalped and dismembered bodies were scattered about the creekside in front of their burning cabin home. A local native American tribe had been held responsible for the attack. There had been so much blood at the site that whatever gore hadn't soaked into the ground flowed down into the creek, turning it crimson. From that day on, Blaudie's Creek became known as Bloody Creek.

The night of the attack, a neighbor at an adjacent farm heard numerous gunshots in the distance and came to investigate, accompanied by his two teenage sons. Things had become tense between the settlers and the indigenous people. Although the sound of gunfire was not uncommon because of hunting, the number of reports told the neighbor there was likely trouble. Unfortunately, by the time they arrived, it was all over.

The gruesome sight was more than the neighbor and his two boys could bear. Someone had slaughtered the entire family. Two of the children, one named Caleb Blaudie, a boy of ten, and his six-year-old sister Emma, had been tomahawked and scalped. The farmer's wife, Emily, had been bludgeoned with a stone-headed club or ax. The attacker removed her arms and legs from her torso, which had been stripped naked. It was apparent she had been sexually violated multiple times in the moments before her death.

Clayton Blaudie and another son, Jacob, a thirteen-year-old boy, managed to shoot three of the savages before they were overwhelmed and hacked to pieces, apparently while they were still alive. Only one member of the family survived to carry on the family name. An older son, Harrison Blaudie, had been away visiting relatives overnight and hadn't been home when the attack came.

Through the centuries that followed, the place had become the stuff of legend. People told dozens of different stories about the massacre, one being more horrifying, fantastic, and more brutal than the last. As often is the case in such tragic events, people tended to let their imaginations run away with them, and then it wasn't very long before the alleged ghost sightings began.

Many locals claimed to have experienced a wide assortment of unexplainable phenomena, such as cold spots along the wooded trails surrounding the creek. Some claimed to have seen shadows moving among the trees. Others said they had heard war whoops, drumming, screams, and cries of pain coming from the darkness.

Martin Clark had heard or read about most of the stories. Since moving to the area several years earlier, he had been fascinated by the place. He had discovered the oddly named site one day while driving around, exploring the area. He had noticed the weathered sign by the side of the highway pointing down along an old dirt and gravel road grown thick with weeds and saplings. He found it incredible that someone gave an actual place such a horrible name, so he researched Bloody Creek. That was when he learned about the massacre and the various alleged ghost stories associated with it. Then, to his surprise, he discovered he had a personal connection to Bloody Creek.

While studying the family tree of Clayton Jackson Blaudie, Martin saw a name he had never imagined he would see. His great-grandmother, Gladys Mayfield, had been married to a Blaudie descendent. That meant Martin himself had descended from the Blaudie line. He was amazed. He stumbled upon Bloody Creek and its fascinating story by sheer accident, only to coincidentally find he had an actual family tie to the horrible tragedy. He shuddered at the realization that the blood running through his veins was the same blood that spilled into the creek so many decades earlier.

Martin was not concerned about the numerous stories and legends surrounding Bloody Creek. He prided himself on being a modern man of the twenty-first century, and as such, he felt He had no time in his life for superstitious mumbo jumbo. However, he was a bit disturbed by something else he had recently uncovered, especially since he now knew he was distantly related to the slain family.

What was bothering him was one account he had read, which claimed that it might have been Clayton Blaudie who had provoked the Indian attack by first shooting two braves who had been trespassing on his property earlier in the day. Another report said that the farmer and his son had killed more than three Indians during the attack, which was initially reported but killed five or six.

Some of the accounts said Blaudie's original murder of the two young braves earlier that fateful day caused the rest of the tribe to seek revenge. And, of course, they had done just that later that evening, losing four or five additional tribesmen in the process. However, in the late 1700s, no one would have considered siding with the native Americans, even if they had known the truth. The attacks on the Blaudie family brought with it a cry for justice in the name of the slain victims. Several weeks later, a local militia rounded up a half dozen braves, took them roped and bound to the town's central square, where they were systematically executed by hanging.

The town only had one gallows sporting one hangman's rope, so each of the tribesmen had to wait his turn to die while watching his brethren dangle by their necks, hands bound behind their backs, legs kicking in the air. One by one, each man was hung, gagging and gasping for his last precious breath. The only thing possibly as unthinkable as the manner of the death itself was the horror of having to watch each man die before you, knowing you were just minutes away from suffering the same horrendous fate.

Yet it was said they bore their fate bravely, not even one breaking down, begging forgiveness, or showing the slightest sign of weakness. They died like proud warriors. They each said silent prayers to their gods of the earth, sea, and sky and never addressed the crowd of white onlookers hungry for their deaths. That is, except for one young brave, the only one among them who knew how to speak in the white man's tongue.

He said to the gathering, "You think it is right to kill us for what happened to the farm man and his people. But he made this happen by killing our brothers."

"Shut yer filthy heathen mouth, Injun. Soon yer neck'll be stretched so long you'll be able to reach the highest apples on the tree. Ha ha," one of the spectators shouted.

Another chimed in, "'Ceptin, you'll be too dead to care."

The crowd broke into raucous laughter. "You tell 'em, Charley," another shouted.

The young warrior ignored their chiding and shouted, "I put a curse upon this town and all your children and all your children's children for all time. If anyone dares to set foot near the place where my brothers died, they will die as the farm man died. Serpents will arise and . . ."

That was when the trap door opened, and the last of the young warriors fell through. He was more fortunate than his predecessors as the impact of the drop and the haphazardly placed knot snapped his neck instantly.

"Ah shucks, Willie. Why'd you go and do something like that fer? We was 'specially hopin' to see this big mouth dance around in the air fer a while," one of the onlookers shouted.

The hangman just shrugged his shoulders with his palms facing upward in an "I don't know" gesture.

Of course, these conversations likely didn't occur and were nothing more than Martin's imaginings of how things must have been back on that fateful day centuries earlier. That was probably why the scene played out more like a cheesy Western movie than what actually might have taken place. However, Martin had read enough witness accounts of the hanging to know one of the braves did speak English and placed a curse on Bloody Creek.

In Martin's opinion, things like curses or hexes fell into the same category as ghosts and legends. They were meaningless in this modern age. Whether he had a blood connection to the Blaudie family or not, he understood he had a burning desire to learn more about this mysterious local hot spot. Today, he was determined to find out exactly what it was about the place that had so many locals on edge.

He pulled the van off the main road onto the dirt and stone road but wouldn't take the chance of driving any further. Then again, he couldn't if he wanted to unless he was driving an ATV or maybe a motorcycle. The road was barely discernible as it was so grown over with tall grass and saplings. He walked past the wooden Bloody Creek Road sign but didn't see the other one, which lay face down on the ground, covered in a blanket of weeds. Had he seen the sign and flipped it over, he might have turned around and driven as far from the horrible place as possible. It held a note which appeared to be written on the sign with a bloody finger. It read, "Death Awaits."

As he began to walk a few hundred feet along the trail, he saw the horrible excuse for a road coming to an end against a forest thick with trees. Of course, it did, he realized. Why hadn't he thought of it sooner? The massacre had happened hundreds of years ago. People stayed away.

Nature had taken over as it always did. The original farm might lie somewhere on the other side of the forest, but it was likely that it, too, had become overgrown.

Martin had no idea why the makeshift road existed or why it ended so abruptly. Someone sometime in the distant past must have started to build the road then, for whatever reason, stopped. Whatever the case, he had to decide whether he would continue onward or turn around and head back. That was when he heard the sound of running water.

"It's the creek," he said to himself, "It has to be the sound of Bloody Creek flowing just a bit further into these woods."

He looked down and noticed a space between some large trees where smaller trees and saplings now grew. It was a place of recent growth, which likely had once been a path. Martin began to push the small trees and branches aside as he moved forward toward the sound of the creek.

After a few hundred feet, he broke through the woods and found himself standing next to the legendary Bloody Creek. A few dozen feet off to his left, Martin could see a low stone wall practically hidden among trees. He knew at once it had to be the remains of the Blaudie homestead. He was likely standing in the same spot where the massacre of his distant relatives had taken place so many decades earlier.

Martin found it only slightly emotional. The fact was everything felt a bit surreal to him. People had been slaughtered and dismembered right where he stood, yet if he hadn't known that, it would have just seemed like another autumn afternoon standing next to a clear, pleasant stream as the leaves changed from green to a lovely bouquet of fall flora. It was simply beautiful, and somehow, that seemed so wrong.

He wasn't sure what exactly he had expected to find here, perhaps the burned-out remains of a dead forest and a creek brown with sludge and decay. Maybe he had imagined there would be a scattering of human bones. After all, the place was supposed to be a site cursed by the dying breath of a doomed savage. He had never expected to see such incredible beauty and such . . . normalcy.

After absorbing everything he saw before him, Martin realized he was more than pleased by what he had found. He decided right there, and then when he returned home, he would investigate and find out if the land was for sale. He had done well for himself in business, and why not spend some of his money to build himself a weekend getaway cabin? This place would be perfect for him to do just that. It would be a special place to come and escape from the rat race. That was when he heard a moaning sound coming from the bushes along the creekside.

"Who . . . who's there? Is anyone there?" Martin asked, "Are you hurt? Do you need help?"

There was no response other than the mournful moaning coming from the underbrush. Martin slowly approached the bushes, being cautious if some poor animal was lying wounded. He was in the woods, after all, and it was more than likely that whatever animal was hiding in those bushes was wild, not someone's pet. It was also possible the animal might be rabid. The more he thought about it, the less he wanted to investigate. Perhaps he should let nature take its course.

However, that wasn't Martin's way. He could never stand around and do nothing while some poor creature was suffering. So, he slowly hunkered down and carefully separated the bushes to see what sort of creature was making the sound and whether or not it was injured. To his surprise, peering into the bushes, there was nothing there, not a single creature of any sort. That was when he noticed the moaning sounds had stopped.

Martin stood and felt the cool autumn breeze begin to blow once more, and it somehow seemed to be even colder down here by the creek. He heard the moaning sound again and felt foolish with the realization it had been the wind blowing through the trees that had made the haunting sounds, nothing more. He let out an involuntary sigh of relief. That was when he felt something ice-cold running up his back and down both of his arms.

"What the Hell . . ." he shouted, but then his voice went silent as the icy chill ran up his throat, paralyzing his vocal cords. His arms and legs were likewise rendered immobile by the numbing coldness. Martin felt something thick, cold yet liquid-like creeping slowly up the front of his neck, then onto his chin, then over his lips. It was as if a snake with skin as cold as a tomb had been crawling along his flesh. Then it rose in front of his face, and he saw the absolute horror of what it was.

It was squirming before his eyes, a blood-red worm-like thing, which appeared to be made mostly of water, but not quite. It was like the water that was thicker and turned crimson. He could see the deep rivulets of red swirling among the clear water. It was almost the consistency of blood. Martin looked outward and saw that the entire creek had turned red. Everywhere along its ruby-stained banks, dozens of the slithering things were emerging from the water and heading his way. The words blood snakes popped into his mind. The thing swaying back and forth in front of his face had no eyes or no mouth, yet Martin felt the horrid thing was not only staring right at him, but it seemed to be looking into his soul and knowing everything about him.

Martin realized this horrid hell-spawned monster would sense the Blaudie blood coursing through his veins. Then he thought of the curse the young Indian brave had reportedly placed on the town as well as all of Blaudie's descendants. As far as Bloody Creek was concerned, he was a Blaudie. Martin opened his mouth to scream, and the crimson serpent slithered inside and down his throat before he had time to close his mouth.

His body went frigid with cold as dozens more of the blood snakes wrapped themselves around his legs while still others climbed onto his arms, and several encircled his neck. Then, as if working in a choreographed dance of destruction, they began to tighten their frigid grips simultaneously. Seconds later, Martin's left arm separated from his body and dropped to the ground. Then, his right arm followed. He could feel the icy serpents tightening on his legs, and he knew they would be next. Mercifully, the blood snake around his neck drew first, and his head dropped to the ground just seconds before his legs were severed.

As the dismembered corpse lay in a puddle of its own thick, chilling blood, the creek sent more blood serpents to pull the remaining pieces of what was once Martin Clark into the water, which was already returning to its pristine clarity. Near the water's edge, the faint sounds of tribal drumming and whooping war cries echoed in the air.

TO BEE OR NOT TO BEE

It was spring cleanup time, a chore Paul never looked forward to but one that had become something of an annual ritual. A ritual, it might be, but a necessary ritual. Paul and his wife Darla prided themselves on their beautiful yard. Their yard was a lush and gorgeous paradise, what the couple considered an oasis, a getaway from the weekly rat race. They sat out on their covered patio every night after work, relaxing the sounds of nature.

However, as with all things worth having, getting their paradise up to speed after a long, cold winter, with its brutal winds and damaging storms, required a ton of spring cleanup and many repairs to their numerous outdoor features. Paul's current yard maintenance job was to repair the top of a treated lumber archway that formed the rear gate entrance to their backyard. Paul had designed and constructed the entrance years earlier, even building the treated lumber gate himself. Paul had covered the top of the arch with a lattice made of treated outdoor wood.

Every year, vines would grow up the sides of the archway, and we're supported on top by this latticework. Darla was the one who had the green thumb and planted the original vine. Paul didn't know a plant from a weed and couldn't recall the name of this vine if his life depended upon it, but he did enjoy watching it grow every year and blossom as it gradually climbed across his archway.

Unfortunately, the many winters and too many prior vines had taken their toll on the lattice. Paul found it broken to pieces beneath the archway. He had trimmed the vine back the previous fall and now had access to the top. Another good thing was the temperature was still in the low fifties, so any bees that might have taken refuge nearby would be sleeping.

Paul was not afraid of bees, nor was he allergic, but for some reason, the bees, which hung around his arch in the summer months, were bothersome. He believed they were called carpenter bees. They were the big black and yellow things that bore holes in the wood for their homes. As far as he knew, they didn't sting, but he had heard stories that they did bite, although he doubted that was true as he had not experienced any bites so far. Besides ruining wooden outdoor structures, the insects were known for their loud buzzing and for dive-bombing anyone who came near the gate.

Fortunately, Paul hardly ever used this entrance, and he would either ignore the pests or swat at any that got too close. The real problem was with the women in his life: his wife, daughters, and granddaughters. They were terrified of all bees, Although Paul had no idea why. He suspected it was something his mother-in-law handed down to his wife, who handed it down to their daughters, who were both presently passing it on to his granddaughters.

Paul looked up at the sky and saw this would be a nice day. Then, he took out his smartphone to check the forecasted temperature for the later part of the day. It reported that by 1:00 pm, the temperature would go up to sixty-five degrees. If that happened, not only would he be likely to be pestered by carpenter bees, but by gnats, flies, yellow jackets, and God only knew what else. It was only 9:30 am, and he could feel the sun on his arms already starting to raise the temperature.

He decided now was the best time to get this project out of the way. He cut three lengths of treated lumber for cross pieces and had a brand-new roll of chicken wire spread across the top. Paul had opted not to use treated lattice again and didn't want to fork out the money for the PVC version of lattice offered at the home centers. He planned to nail the three short two-by-four strips across the top framework, then cut and fasten the chicken wire on top of the lumber. It might not be beautiful, but it would end up covered in vines within a month anyway.

He laughed to himself as he read the label on the bound wire. It read, "Poultry Netting." Paul thought this was a bit pretentious as he had never referred to the product as anything but chicken wire. He suddenly recalled that old Grey Poupon Dijon mustard commercial from the 1980s where one limousine pulled up next to another limousine, the windows rolled down, and one rich guy asked the other, "Pardon me, do you have any Grey Poupon?" Then the other rich guy says, "But of course."

Instead of Grey Poupon, Paul imagined the one rich guy asking, "Pardon me, do you have any poultry netting?" He had to chuckle at how his mind worked and at the most peculiar times.

He grabbed a piece of lumber, his hammer, and some nails. Climbing his step ladder, Paul began nailing the first crosspiece onto the top of the archway. As he did, he heard a faint and intermittent buzzing, sounding as if coming from far away. Then, he saw what he thought were small leaves fluttering down from the archway to the ground. When he climbed down the ladder to retrieve the second piece of wood, he was surprised by what he saw.

Six or seven carpenter bees were on the ground, all alive and moving. They appeared to be waking up as if from a dormant state. The temperature was still too cool for them to awaken fully. Paul realized as the temperature climbed later in the day, however, they would become very active. He decided this was not going to happen on his watch.

Paul began stepping on one bee after another, squashing each one. Some of them took two stomps to die completely as they lay with broken wings and guts oozing out of them, still twitching and buzzing. Paul was surprised to see so many of the creatures in one place together as he had always believed this type of bee to be solitary. They didn't build huge nests or swarm as other bees or hornets did. They tended to bore holes in wood to build tiny homes where they lived alone or laid their eggs. Perhaps that was what these were, the results of a cluster of hatched eggs.

Then he noticed one other bee that he had missed earlier or had just fallen from above. It appeared larger than the others. Perhaps it was the female, and these others had been her offspring. Whatever the case, she was about to join her children in the great BEE-yond. Again, he chuckled to himself as he raised his foot to squash the last bee. That was when everything went wrong.

A loud, piercing scream came from somewhere in the distance. It was so loud it made Paul lift his hands to cover his ears. It was both mournful, yet Paul could sense its anger simultaneously. It seemed to grow louder by the second. He looked down and realized the sound was impossibly coming from the remaining bee. The thing appeared to be looking right at him as it began to rise from the ground.

Paul backed away, certain now the creature was going to attack him. However, he didn't see the remaining two pieces of wood on the ground and tripped over them, falling backward. He crashed to the ground, feeling the wind knocked out of him. His head ached where it had smashed against a bed of decorative stones, another of his earlier projects. As he lay motionless, waiting to get his wind back, he tried to assess what damage he had suffered.

He could feel a trickle of warm liquid creeping down the side of his face and realized he had cut something, his face or, most likely, his head. His right ankle squealed with pain when he tried to move it. Hopefully, it was only a bad sprain. His entire right side likewise burned with pain from his fall. As he lay on the ground, Paul heard a familiar buzzing sound and saw the bee, the very same bee he was sure, hovering in the air right just inches in front of his face. He tried to swat the creature away with his hand but found he was still too disoriented, and his feeble attempt did nothing to scare the bee away.

He slowly tried to get up. As he did, he felt a stabbing pain in his ankle and knew he had broken it. He howled with agony. As he did, he felt something fly over his lips, its buzzing wings flitting first against the inside of his mouth, then the back of his mouth, and finally deep down in his throat. The bee! That accursed creature was inside him, in his throat.

Bolts of electric agony shot up from his throat, and Paul knew instantly what the thing was doing. It was chewing a hole in his windpipe the same way it bored into solid wood. But his flesh would be much easier to tunnel through than wood. Paul gagged and tried to cough up the vile creature but couldn't. He crammed his fingers into the back of his throat, hoping to aggravate his gag reflex.

I'll coat you in puke and barf you out, he thought angrily.

Then, a notion appeared in his mind. It was not so much a voice speaking to him but an understanding. In essence, it told him, "No, today, human, today you will die for killing my family."

Paul knew such a thing was impossible, yet he could feel his throat close and his airways constricting as the pain in his throat increased to unimaginable levels. As he lay on the ground, struggling for a breath, he could see across the distance to the place where the other bees lay, the ones he killed. Soon, the world began to fade, then finally darkened as he breathed his last.

The body lay where it had fallen, only now its flesh had a dusky hue. Its lips, which now hung open as they had been moments earlier, were bluish-purple. After a few seconds, a distant buzzing sound could be heard. Moments later, a female carpenter bee crawled across those now-dead lips and flew up to the highest point on the archway, where it immediately began the job of boring a new hole in the wood for its home.

ART'S WORK

"A man paints with his brains and not with his hands."
—MICHELANGELO

"A beautiful body perishes, but a work of art dies not."
—LEONARDO DA VINCI

"The purpose of art is washing the dust of daily life off our souls."
—PABLO PICASSO

"True art is characterized by an irresistible urge
in the creative artist."
—ALBERT EINSTEIN

Arthur sat quietly in his spacious living room, looking from wall to wall at the various works of art hanging there. They were of so many different and varied styles, yet all seemed to fit well into the decorating scheme of the place. He remembered how his wife Sonia loved these pieces and often would spend hours showing off her art to their guests. These works were her artwork, not works of the famous or the infamous, but the work she had created herself. Perhaps they were not museum quality or even worth attempting to sell, but they had been hers, and that made each one of them irreplaceable to him.

Sonia was a true artist, a creator. Not only could she come up with her unique styles and artistic methods, but she would also often scour the internet, looking for new and exciting techniques. Then, she would use these techniques to produce almost every piece of artwork currently displayed in their home. Arthur would often assist her, but unfortunately, he didn't have much of an imagination, and he always felt he had no artistic talent whatsoever.

But he loved Sonia with all his heart, and as he looked around the room, he felt proud that he had at least been able to contribute in some small way to the beautiful pieces hanging on the walls. However, this act of studying his beloved wife's work was always bittersweet. It made him feel extremely happy to see the fruits of their combined labor while simultaneously shrouding him in a black fog of melancholy. What else should he expect now that his beautiful Sonia was dead, her cremains spread among her flowers in their garden?

He looked over at one particular painting, a black and white geometric patterned piece on the far wall. It was six feet by six feet in size, resembling a design made by a giant Spirograph machine he had once played with as a small child. The painting's bright white, elliptical shapes overlapped and flowed in and out of each other, standing out incredibly against the coal-black background.

Sonia had gotten the idea to create the piece from a video she had seen on the internet of a couple doing similar work and decided she wanted to try the technique herself. So, as always, she recruited Arthur to assist. First, he cut a six-foot square of plywood with one side smoothly finished. Next, he brush-painted it flat black. Anticipating the final geometric patterns, Sonia had instructed him to apply the paint in a circular, swirling motion so that when observed up close, any brush strokes would help to enhance the elliptical patterns. That was another reason Sonia was the artist; she always thought of things like this. Arthur covered their garage floor with a plastic tarp and suspended a quart can of white paint on a rope from the ceiling, hanging about six inches directly over the black square he had painted. Again, at Sonia's suggestion, he offset the can somewhat from the center of the square.

Now, it was time for Sonia to take over. She held the can away from the square while Arthur first drilled a small hole in the bottom of the can. Then, as Sonia covered the hole with her finger, he drilled another hole in the top of the can, which would allow a thin stream of paint to begin flowing once Sonia removed her finger from the bottom. Sonia took careful aim and sent the can slowly flying in an arc over the tarp and black square. They watched in amazement as the swirling paint created geometric results on the black canvas below.

That had been two years earlier and had been one of the last few pieces she had made before . . . before the unimaginable tragedy had happened. Arthur had been away on business for a few days when that low-life bastard had broken into their home, raped and beaten his precious Sonia to death, then robbed their home of whatever he could find. They were not wealthy people by any means, but they did have a few nice things of value. The murderer had even taken a few of Sonia's works of art.

That was how the man, one John Steven Harding, had been caught. Police had apprehended him after he had attempted to pawn Sonia's jewelry and her paintings. The pawnshop had sensed something dishonest in Harding and had immediately contacted the police. Not to suggest the owner was opposed to purchasing less than legal items, but there was something so far off about Harding that the owner said just being in the room with the strange man made his skin crawl.

Eventually, Harding was arrested, charged, and brought to trial. Unfortunately, as is sometimes the case, Harding was released on a legal technicality, which Arthur didn't quite understand. It drove Arthur mad with rage, realizing the man who had raped and murdered his precious Sonia could be walking the streets as a free man.

Now, as he sat in the silence of their home, Arthur's memories switched focus, and he recalled the night several months ago when he had finally gotten his revenge. After carefully planning, he had captured Harding, brought him to his home, and dragged his unconscious body down the steps to his basement. The hours that followed were so brutal and so incredibly savage that Arthur could scarcely believe he had been responsible for such a blood bath. He had tortured the bound man relentlessly for hours, doing things he would have never imagined himself capable of doing. Then, after bringing unimaginable agony to the murderer, Arthur ended his barbaric session by unceremoniously slitting the man's throat. Being the neat and organized person he was, Arthur had spread a plastic tarp on the floor to catch any evidence. This proved especially helpful when he began systematically dismembering the corpse for proper disposal. There had been so much blood, quarts of the stuff, what seemed like gallons.

Arthur recalled sitting on a chair staring at the bloody tarp recalled how he and Sonia had made that black and white geometric piece of artwork. It felt so insanely surrealistic for him to be sitting in a room full of his victim's body parts among buckets of blood while thinking of the beautiful piece of art he and Sonia had created. Then, he was caught completely off guard with a revelation. For the first time in his life, Arthur found himself inspired by an incredibly creative, artistic idea.

Now, months later, he sat in his living room, a man alone with nothing left in his life but Sonia's artwork and his memories. The police had never found Harding's remains and never would; Arthur had seen to that. They had, of course, been suspicious of Arthur, not that he cared as he felt he no longer had any reason to live anyway. They had even stopped by many times to question him and have a forensic team search his home but had never found a spec of evidence. He had to chuckle to himself at how close the police had come to the evidence they so desperately wanted, enough evidence to send him to the death house, yet they never even saw it.

On the wall next to his and Sonia's black-and-white geometric work was another similar work. It was on a matching six-foot square, but this painting had a bright white background instead of a white pattern on a black background. The similar Spirograph-like pattern was once a deep ruby red; now, it seemed to have faded to a reddish-brown color. Arthur had to smile whenever he looked at the result of his only artistic inspiration, what he liked to call Art's work.

FRIENDS

"An insincere and evil friend is more to be feared
than a wild beast; a wild beast may wound your body,
but an evil friend will wound your mind."
—UNKNOWN

"A quarrel between friends, when made up,
adds a new tie to friendship."
—SAINT FRANCIS DE SALES

"It's OK to argue with your friends. Guys can do it better than
girls, usually, but if you ever get into a fight with a true friend or a
spouse or a boyfriend, get it out, fight, be angry for five minutes,
and then move past it. Don't let it fester; don't hold a grudge. If
you do, that's when it will get worse and worse."
—IKE BARINHOLTZ

The ceiling fan spun in lazy circles above, doing little, if anything, to
relieve the oppressive heat and unbearable humidity. It was one of those
late summer days when even thinking could make you break out in a
sweat. Clayton sat sprawled on his wicker armchair, his arms dangling
over the sides, his legs spread wide. Thinking was the last thing he
wanted to do for the moment. Clad only in an athletic tee shirt and
boxers and positioned directly under the fan, he was doing all he could
to catch every bit of moving air the device could produce.

On a table off to his right were the remnants of several of his favorite summer drinks. These were drinks of the adult variety, that is. He knew the last thing he needed to stay cool was alcohol, no matter what icy form it took, but he also knew its mind-numbing properties would do wonders to help him block out not only the inhospitable temperatures but also thoughts about what he had done.

He was not proud of what had happened, or more specifically, what he had allowed to happen, but neither could he take complete blame for it either. It was partly Ian's fault. Ian had been his best friend since childhood. How could he have let this happen? Not only had Ian created the situation, but he had caused it to escalate from a minor misunderstanding into a full-blown nuclear meltdown. It was now difficult for Clayton to comprehend that they had once been life-long friends and partners. Not partners in the sexual sense but in the business sense. They had been two men who were like brothers and loved each other like brothers. Then again, Cain and Able had been brothers, hadn't they?

As he baked in the afternoon heat, Clayton thought about how he would handle the mess in which he now found himself. He didn't want to think; it was too damned hot to think. All he wanted to do was to drink himself into oblivion, with the hopes that when he awoke, things might be different. Or at least, he might have a solution to his dilemma. At present, the only light he could see at the end of his life's tunnel was the ceiling light in the state's death chamber as they injected him with the legendary needle.

He knew he had no choice but to do something soon. This ungodly heat was breaking records, and his house had poor air conditioning at best. By itself, this would have been more than enough of a problem. But when you added in the fact that his former best friend's body was rolled up in a blood-soaked sheet in his cellar, things got a bit more complicated.

Clayton was thankful he lived on a large chunk of land, far away from everything and everyone. Any noise they may have made would go unnoticed. It also might take a few days before anyone missed Ian and came inquiring. He knew it would only be a matter of time. The authorities would have no difficulty associating Ian with him since they had been business partners, after all. Hopefully, by the time they did, he would have gotten rid of the body and come up with a plausible story, one with all the details worked out. He'd have to be sure he had all his tees crossed and all his i's dotted, as they say.

He had already taken preliminary steps to cover his tracks. Clayton had shut off Ian's cell phone as well as his own. He left his phone in the kitchen, then he drove Ian's car into the city, to one of the worst neighborhoods where he knew someone would quickly steal it. Once there, he had turned Ian's phone back on. After wiping it and the car down to eliminate fingerprints and DNA, he ran out to the main street and caught a gypsy cab to an upscale restaurant in the nicer part of town. Once there, he had a meal, making sure to converse with the server and leave a large tip. This way, he was sure to be remembered.

He made a point of having three strong drinks. Next, he asked his server to call a cab for him as he didn't have his cell phone with him. He said he didn't feel comfortable driving after drinking. As soon as the taxi dropped him off at home, he turned on his phone and called Ian. He didn't leave a message with the first call. Nor did he leave one with the second one he made a half-hour later.

Finally, after another half hour, he let the phone ring to voice mail and left a message, sounding as upbeat and confident as possible. He said, "Ian, my man. It's Clay, Bro. I've been trying to get through to you. This is like my tenth time calling, so I figured I better leave a message. Call me, Dude. I have to discuss boring business crap with you, but it's all good, so call me anytime."

Clayton figured if the cops found Ian's phone, it would be good to have that friendly message there for them. Plus, if they checked phone records, they'd see where Clayton called from, which was his home as it should be. If things worked out, someone would steal Ian's phone and the car long before he got home. There were still some holes in his story he had yet to work out, such as if he took a cab home, that meant his car should still be at the restaurant, but his car was at home. He'd have to work that out later, he decided.

More importantly, he had to figure out what to do with the body for now. But it was too damned hot to worry about that. Ian's body would have to wait. When Clayton returned home, his clothes were sticking to him. He decided to take a nice shower, make another call to Ian's phone, leave another message, and then get completely wasted. That was how he ended up on the porch in his underwear, drinking alcoholic beverages while trying to cool his family jewels under the ceiling fan.

After a bit, he felt the vodka he had used to lace his iced fruit juice working on him just as he had planned it would. He no longer thought of Ian or how he had crushed his best friend's skull with a cast-iron skillet. He no longer saw himself falling on Ian and strangling him until his eyes bugged out of his skull, and his face turned dusky gray. Now he just thought of . . . nothing, he thought of nothing whatsoever. The alcohol did its job, and he drifted off to sleep.

Clayton woke up several hours later, drenched in sweat, his arms and legs numb from lack of circulation, having hung limply over the sides of the chair for God only knew how long. He tried to sit up but couldn't, so he rolled to the side, and his body flopped down onto the gray boards of the porch. He felt like a fish out of water as he flipped about, doing his best to get blood back into his appendages. Soon, his struggle paid off, but that was when the real problems started.

His arms and legs felt like an acupuncturist from Hell was piercing them. The feeling of hundreds of pins raced through him while his blood found its way back into his arms and legs. After several more agonizing minutes, he began to feel somewhat normal, at least good enough to try to stand up. He crawled on hands and knees back to his wicker chair and pulled himself up to something vaguely resembling a standing position. He held onto the arm of the chair for support as the final waves of discomfort passed. He still felt out of sorts and a bit tipsy from whatever alcohol remained in his system.

Then he recalled why he had drunk so much and why he had fallen asleep in the first place. It was Ian, or more accurately, Ian's body. It was still in his cellar, rolled in a bedsheet, waiting for him to dispose of it before it began to rot and stink, which Clayton suspected would not be very long despite the cooler temperatures down below.

So . . . whatever to do, whatever to do. Clayton could bury the body out in the field, but cadaver dogs would likely find it if things came to that. He knew if he were considered a suspect, the police would bring such resources. He could chop the body up and run it through his wood chipper, but that would make a royal mess and produce more DNA evidence than he needed. He could wall the body up in his cellar, but again, the cadaver dogs would have no trouble sniffing it out there, either. That was when he realized he should have put the corpse in the backseat of Ian's car. When the thief stole the car, it would have been up to him to get rid of the corpse. Unfortunately, that ship had sailed.

Clayton wondered if he should have just called the police and told them he had killed Ian in self-defense. After all, Ian had come at him with a butcher knife he had pulled from the wood block on the kitchen counter. Clayton had no choice but to defend himself. He had grabbed a cast iron skillet from the stovetop and clobbered Ian in the face, knocking him unconscious to the kitchen floor. Had he stopped there, things would have likely worked out in his favor.

Instead, he wrapped his fingers around his former friend's throat and strangled him to death. Ian had even woken up for an instant to find Clayton squeezing the life out of him. But it was too late at that point, as Ian was too weak to fight back, and Clayton had a strength born of homicidal rage. No, it was far too late to consider getting the police involved. He was going to have to figure a way out of this mess himself. Clayton decided to go down into the cellar and check on the corpse's condition.

The corpse, he thought to himself. Not *Ian* or *him* or *Ian's body* but *the corpse*. He had already started to think of the remains more distantly and clinically. Somehow, that seemed wrong on so many levels. He felt Ian deserved better than that. Then again, Clayton deserved better than to be up to his ears in trouble, yet here he was. He remembered an expression his grandfather often said, "When you're up to your chin in crap, don't make waves."

He had no idea why he thought of that now or what the Hell it had to do with his current situation. Other than the fact that he was currently up to his chin in feces at the moment.

As he walked through the doorway to the cellar, Clayton flipped on the light switch only to find the light not working. That was strange, as it had worked earlier in the day when he had dragged Ian's body down the steps. By now, even after flipping the switch multiple times, the cellar remained dark.

Clayton reached over and grabbed the flashlight he kept on a shelf at the top of the stairs. He pressed the button and was happy to find the batteries still working. Holding the handrail, he made his way carefully down into the darkness of the cellar. And it certainly was a cellar, not to be confused with a basement. His home was an old farmhouse, and this cellar had a dirt floor.

He shone his light over at the side of the cellar where he had placed the corpse. Clayton could see the bloody sheet right where he had left it. However, something seemed very wrong with the covering. It seemed to lay flat on the dirt floor, where it should still have had the form of Ian's body under it. As he got closer, Clayton hesitantly grabbed one of the corners of the sheet and raised it slightly to look underneath for the body. There was none to see.

That was impossible. Clayton yanked the sheet free, only to discover no dead body below it. That was when he saw the dark, round shape in the dirt. It was a hole that appeared to be large enough for a man. That is, of course, a living man, not a dead one. As Clayton got closer to the hole, he could see a tunnel of sorts in the shadows made by his flashlight. But that, too, was impossible. Ian had been dead; Clayton was sure of that. But even if Ian somehow had been alive, he never would have been able to burrow so deep into the ground as to tunnel his way out of the cellar. There would have been no need to do so anyway since Clayton hadn't locked the cellar door. If Ian had awoken alive, all he would have had to do was walk up the stairs and leave. So, why was this hole here, and why a tunnel? That was when the flashlight started to dim and flicker.

"Damn batteries," Clayton swore. Why hadn't he brought down his smartphone? It had a flashlight built into it. A lot of good it did him sitting up on the kitchen table. As the light dimmed, Clayton knew he would be in darkness in a few seconds. He turned to head toward the steps. That was when he felt an icy cold sensation tightening around his ankle.

Clayton turned and pointed his almost useless flashlight down at his foot and, to his shock and horror, saw a mottled gray hand clamped tightly around his ankle. The hand had emerged from the hole in the dirt floor. In the dwindling off-and-on strobe-light-like effect of his flashlight, he saw Ian, dead Ian, impossibly dragging himself up out of the hole.

The corpse's face was ashen and dusky gray. Its eyes were filmed over and stitched with petechial veins from his strangulation. The most horrible sight was his wide-open snapping jaws filled with chipped and broken teeth. Clayton hadn't recalled Ian's teeth having looked so bad in life. Perhaps they had broken when he had struck Ian with the cast iron skillet. Whatever the cause, they now looked sharp, deadly, and far too jagged.

Clayton tried to shake himself free of the Ian creature's grasp but soon felt the thing's other hand clamp tightly around his remaining ankle. He fell face-first to the dirt floor, tasting soil in his mouth and smelling the musty earth up in his nostrils. Pain shot through his face from cuts he knew he had gotten on his lips and face. Clayton reached out and grabbed for anything that might help him but felt his fingers digging uselessly into the soft soil of the cellar floor. He had lost his flashlight during the fall, and it lay outside of his reach, shining back toward him with what meager light remained, illuminating his face as he was dragged slowly backward. His fingers dug uselessly into the soft dirt of the cellar floor as the monster, which had once been his best friend, pulled him back into whatever Hell the creature had in store for him.

ARBORGORK

"Man is not above nature, but in nature."
—ERNST HAECKEL

"Look deep into nature, and then you will
understand everything better."
—ALBERT EINSTEIN

The estate property was enormous. Ethan couldn't believe one person could own something so vast. What had she said it was, over five hundred acres of woodlands? It was incredible. He was amazed by all of this land and the beautiful mansion sitting smack dab in the middle of it, surrounded by several acres of lush, manicured lawn. It was intoxicating to think that he might have a real shot at becoming part of all of this. He knew he would have to play his cards right to make that happen, and he most certainly did intend to do just that.

Ethan Somers was what young people would call a player, something older folks might call a playboy. But in reality, he was nothing more than a high-end con man. He loved women, and for reasons he never bothered to question, women loved him. More importantly, women loved to give him things, not just to give of themselves sexually, but to give him material things. They gave him cars, jewelry, and expensive vacations to exotic places. Some had even paid to put him up in high-priced hotels and apartments. You see, Ethan made a point always to target wealthy women, and he had the looks and charisma to do just that.

Two of the most important things these women gave Ethan were their trust and money. Over the years, Ethan had managed to bilk dozens of these unsuspecting women out of millions of dollars, promising to invest their funds in bogus schemes, all of which ended with the women losing their investments while simultaneously filling Ethan's offshore bank accounts. Once he had accomplished this, Ethan would disappear, lay low for a few months, and then reappear in a different city with another name and a different back story. Then, he would immediately begin looking for another wealthy woman to victimize.

During his life, he had gone by names such as Edward Sands, Eli Santino, and Eric Spencer, to name a few. Now, he was Ethan Somers. He always tried to stick with the same initials. This was not only because it made his false names easier to remember but also because it eliminated the need to alter any of his personal monogrammed items. In Ethen's opinion, these various items brought with them a sense of proud financial accomplishment. That was all that mattered to him.

Ethan Somers lived the lavish life of a jet-setting man of the world, all on money stolen from his numerous lovers. However, he was smart enough to understand the clock was ticking. Ethan was getting older, and sooner or later, he'd have to give up his lifestyle in favor of something much safer and more . . . dare he say . . . permanent. And maybe, just maybe, this latest conquest would be precisely the sort of payday he needed.

Her name was Lyla. He had started charming her a month or so earlier, and as always, he was careful not to introduce sex into the equation until he felt it was the right moment. Ethan liked to make the woman think it was her idea to start the physical aspect of their relationship. That was the first step in his building their trust. Lyla had crossed that bridge by their second date, practically throwing herself at him. She had proved to be one of the most unique and physically challenging lovers Ethan had ever experienced. Perhaps he was getting older sooner than he thought.

Once they had gotten beyond the physical, it was time for Ethan to begin forming an emotional attachment with Lyla. Being a sociopath with no genuine empathy for others, Ethan had mastered mimicking a variety of emotions, such as caring and loving, by watching movies as well as paying close attention to the people around him. He had become quite good at it. Soon, Lyla was telling him things about herself and her past she never usually would have told anyone she had known for such a short time.

She told Ethan she was the widow of a wealthy investment banker who had been married more to his job than to her. Ethan, of course, feigned sympathy as she told her tale. She said her husband had "died with his boots on," indicating he had keeled over at his desk, falling face-first onto his keyboard as the stock market reports crawled across several large wall-mounted televisions in front of him.

Lyla had admitted to Ethan that she had come from nothing and had used her charm and beauty to snag her wealthy husband. She had also told him she was a Wicken. He didn't quite understand all of what that Wicken stuff was about, but if he was correct, it meant she was some sort of witch. Not the broomstick-riding, pointy black hat, and cloak-wearing, *Wizard of Oz*, "I'll get you my pretty" type of witch, but someone who worships mother nature, plants, and trees or some other weird crap like that.

He didn't care about any of that tree-hugging stuff, and why should he? All he needed to know was she was gorgeous, great in the sack, and richer than King freakin' Midas. Anything else he could work around until he managed to gain enough of her trust to work his way into her bank accounts. He'd decided he'd continue to take his time cultivating this one; there was too much cashola riding on this deal to screw it up. *What was that old song? Whatever Lola wants, Lola gets? That could work just as efficiently for Lyla*, he thought. *Whatever Lyla wants . . . yadda, yadda, yadda, and so on.*

Ethan was presently sitting on the back patio near the luxurious outdoor kitchen overlooking the swimming pool and hot tub, looking out at the property's thick forest. He was wearing nothing more on this warm summer morning than a pair of boxers and slip-on canvas sneakers. He had just finished eating the delicious breakfast Lyla had made for him and was washing it down with some fruit drink infused with a bit of vodka.

Lyla had informed him that she needed to leave for a few hours to take care of some money business in the city and suggested that Ethan make himself at home and relax until she returned. He liked the sound of that for several reasons. The first reason was that when Lyla told him about the "money business," she became comfortable discussing financial matters with him. This revelation was a definite sign of her starting to trust him. Ethan knew trust was essential to Lyla and had to chuckle to himself since building such trust was crucial to his profession, that is, if you could call swindling a job.

Before she left, Lyla had requested, "All I ask is that you stay here around the house and don't go out into the forest. It's a big area. It's easy to get turned around and lost out there, and there are lots of wild animals living in the woods."

Ethan had said, "To be honest, Lyla, I have no interest in the forest whatsoever. However, if I did, I do have a cell phone and could call for help if I ran into a problem."

"Look at your phone, Ethan," she suggested.

He did, and after seeing it, he said with embarrassment, "Whoops. No service. I guess we are really out in the middle of nowhere."

"True. But remember, there is a landline inside the house if you need to call anyone. I want to get a sat phone one of these days. Those are supposed to be great for places like this. So, look, I gotta go but promise I won't be long, no more than two or three hours. Make yourself at home. Watch TV, swim in the pool. *Mi Casa su Casa.*"

"Works for me," Ethan said agreeably. He had every intention of making her "Casa" his "Casa" as soon as possible.

"But please, don't go exploring out in the woods, Ethan. It can be dangerous. I didn't mention it before because I don't like to discuss past lovers, but that's how my last boyfriend died. He was lost in the woods and became injured. Eventually, he died alone in those woods. I don't want that to happen to you. I think we have something special here, Ethan. Now, can I trust you to stay here near the house while I'm gone? You remember how I told you trust is extremely important to me."

"Of course, you can trust me," Ethan replied, "Trust is my middle name; Ethan Trust . . . Somers." Oops, he had almost said Sanders, one of his previous surnames. That wouldn't have been good. Then he thought of how many times he had used that same "Trust" middle name joke on God only knew how many women right before he relieved them of their life's savings.

Now he sat sipping his drink while Lyla was gone, off doing her business, her money business. Ca-ching baby! Ethan was sitting and contemplating the five hundred wooded acres surrounding him. Against his better judgment, he was beginning to get curious. Why did she have to mention not going into the woods? If she had said nothing, he probably would have been content to sit by the pool and chill until she returned, but she had to go and tell him to stay out of the woods. For Pete's sake, that was like telling someone not to think of the color red. Once the thought was in your head, you could think of nothing else. And now he was thinking of the forest. Why had she told him to stay out of the woods? What might she be hiding out there?

Maybe he should just listen to her and stay where he was. This gig was a great money opportunity with fantastic potential. He should at least play along for a while until he found a way to start leeching off some of this wealth. It was apparent she was crazy about him and trusted him implicitly. This con would likely be easier than most of his others. All he had to do was play along for a while. Yet, he couldn't help thinking about the woods. It was almost like someone or something was calling to him, urging him to come into the forest and see. See what? This feeling was a bizarre sensation for Ethan to have. He was usually in control, yet this damned curiosity became so strong.

From where he sat, he could see what appeared to be a small opening in the woods between two dense areas thick with trees. It looked like a path into the forest, but he couldn't be sure from this far away. The pull of curiosity was becoming unbearable. What was it about that forest? Lyla had said she was a Wicken, some sort of tree-hugging nature worshipper or something like that. Maybe that was why she wanted him to stay away. Perhaps she had some freaky geeky Wicken church or altar set up out there in the woods. Now Ethan was becoming extremely curious.

He finished his alcohol-laced fruit drink, wiped his mouth with his napkin, and decided he had to know what sort of secrets Lyla was hiding. It was a warm summer morning, and Ethan wondered for a moment if he should get dressed, at least put on jeans and a shirt, but figured what the Hell. They were in the middle of nowhere, surrounded by woods. He could walk naked into the woods, and one would see him. Besides, he had no intention of going too far into the forest. If Lyla did have an altar or shrine out there, it wouldn't be very far in. He was sure there was no way she would venture far on her own.

Finally, Ethan's curiosity got the better of him, and he made his way past the pool and out the pool gate, then down a hill and across the massive lawn, heading straight for the path he had seen from the patio. He was surprised at how long it took to reach the edge of the forest. He turned around and looked back at the mansion, now appearing so far away. Ethan realized he would have to be sure not to lose track of time. He knew it took about a half-hour to get to the city from the estate. That meant another half-hour return trip. If her appointment lasted an hour and she stopped at a store or two, that might buy him another two hours.

He figured he could run back and then hop naked into the pool to cool off. If he were lucky, that was where Lyla would find him and how she would find him when she returned. That would be precisely what she would expect from him. Ethan shook his head in disbelief as he took a final look at the mansion. This unbelievable fortune would all be his very shortly. He turned back to the forest and stepped onto the dirt path.

Within a few seconds, he realized Lyla was right. This forest was so dense with such high, thick trees that just twenty or thirty yards in it had become extremely dark and disorienting. He was still on the path and could still see the opening to the meadow behind him, looking like a tiny open door leading from a darkened room into a brightly lit space. He knew it couldn't possibly be as far behind him as it appeared to be because he hadn't been walking that long. He also realized if he left the path in this black world, he'd never make it back. No wonder Lyla's former lover died in this Hellish place. It had become quite chilly now out of the warming rays of the morning sun, especially clad as he was only in boxers and thin sneakers.

Ethan saw a dim light ahead, where the path turned to the right. It must be a place where the treetops were thinner, and sunlight was allowed to sneak through. As he navigated the curve, he saw the opening behind him fall from view. However, he was still on the path, and as long as he stayed on that path, he believed he would find his way back. At least, he hoped he was right about that.

Ethan walked slowly and cautiously around the curve and, to his surprise, found that it did indeed stop at a clearing surrounded by giant trees thickly populated in a circle around the clearing. In the center of the clearing was a large, flat, round slab of black rock with dozens of blood-red unlit candles melted fast to its surface around its circumference. This was it! Ethan had been right about Lyla. This place was her church, shrine, and altar, right here in the middle of this dense forest.

Then Ethan saw something that made his blood run cold. Glistening in the limited sunlight atop the slab were brownish-purple blotches. He knew immediately those could be nothing but dried blood patches. Was this some sort of sacrificial altar? He was sure something had died on that slab. The question was whether it was an animal or a human. He knew how ridiculous the idea sounded; humans sacrificed on an altar to what? To some forest God? To some tree deities?

From the shadows behind him, Ethan heard a low moan like that of a wounded animal in pain. A ray of light broke through the trees and illuminated one tree in particular. Its top was gone, leaving a stump about six feet tall. It appeared as if someone had skinned off some of the tree's bark to carve something into it. He walked closer and immediately wished he hadn't.

What he saw was beyond anything Ethan had ever imagined, unlike any nightmarish image his late-night pepperoni pizza binges had ever managed to insinuate itself into his dreams. It was a tree, a vine-engulfed tree, yet it was not. It was a man, yet it was not. It was somehow impossibly both.

At its base, it was something so unimaginably hideous it was difficult for his mind to wrap itself around the sight. It was as if someone had carved a replica of the upper half of a human male into the tree, with its lower half bleeding into the bark while this other half extended three feet up the length of the tree stump.

Then, to Ethan's horror, it was apparent that this body was no mere carving, no detailed sculpture, no bizarre work of some perverse artist's imaginings. Ethan could see this image, this sculpture of sorts, wasn't a carving at all. This hideous abomination was the body of a man, the actual flesh and blood upper half of a man somehow infused into the trunk of the tree.

The thing was impossibly growing out of the wooden solidity of the tree itself. Long serpentine vines as thick as two inches in diameter entwined the human-like torso, holding it tight to the tree's trunk. The thing's arms reached upward along the tree and were bound to it by thin snake-like branches.

Ethan was horrified to see how, in places, the vines that resembled branches penetrated the man's flesh, burrowing deep inside his body, leaving a raised pink ring of skin where the flesh met the vine. He could see places where the vines had slithered just below the surface, visible by the raised skin covering the invading vine.

As is the nature of all creeping plants, the vines had found their way back out of the body through the man's various orifices. One particularly thick, pointed vine protruded from his mouth, wrapping itself up along the left side of his head. Other, thinner vines were slithering from his nostrils and ears, proceeding to wrap themselves tightly against the man's flesh before finding their way back to the tree.

The man, if it could still be considered a man, had his eyes closed, and despite the thick phallus-like vine emerging from his mouth, the corners of his lips seemed to be turned up slightly with an unexplainable appearance of satisfaction and comfort. How any living creature could feel comfort in such a situation was beyond Ethan's comprehension.

Ethan was hoping against all hopes that all of this was a terrible nightmare, and at some point, he would awaken in a cold sweat, which he would welcome like a lost lover. What the hell was this hideous thing anyway? That was when the heinous creature before him opened its eyes.

In horror, Ethan first felt his stomach clench, then sensed the warmth and smelled the foul stench of his urine as it ran down his bare legs and puddled in his sneakers. If he were asleep on the deck and dreaming, he would have a nasty mess to clean up whenever he awoke.

The man-thing in the tree never looked directly at Ethan, and he suspected the creature might not be able to. Its eyes seemed to roll around aimlessly like those of a blind man. But they had opened, which might mean the thing was still impossibly alive and might have heard Ethan.

Ethan said, feeling beyond stupid and equally ill at ease, "Um . . . Hello?"

The man/tree thing's eyes continued to roll around as if unknowing or simply unable to respond.

Ethan tried again, "Ah . . . are . . . are you alright? I mean, . . . who or what are you?"

The creature still did not speak. Then again, how could it speak with a massive vine growing from its mouth? Ethan began to hear a low humming inside his head as if someone had just turned on an old transistor radio, not tuned to any particular station. The sound was very slowly increasing in volume. Then, among the static humming inside his head, he thought he heard a single word emerge. That word was "Arbor," something or other. At first, he thought he had heard "Arborcort," and in his mind, he questioned that name as it made little sense. Then he heard the word repeated much louder and much clearer, "Arborgork." But he had heard it, and although he understood the pronunciation, it still made little sense to him, at least in part.

He understood the "Arbor" portion of the name since the creature he saw consisted primarily of a tree. As a kid, Ethan had been a contributor to the Arbor Day Foundation and had sent them a donation. He had received a few saplings in the mail he planted in the woods near his childhood home.

But the second part of the word might have been "gork." He remembered the slang word "gork," which meant something like somebody who was brain-dead, like someone in a coma or something like that. It was often unkindly used to describe some terminally ill patient whose brain was essentially nonfunctioning and whose body was kept alive by machines and being force-fed nutrients. Of course, people often used the word to insult the so-called normal individuals who seemed too stupid to be so.

Yeah, that certainly did describe this pitiful creature he was now seeing. But where had that word, that name Arborgork come from? Ethan shifted his stance and felt the wetness in his sneakers from his involuntary urination had cooled and became quite uncomfortable. Likewise, the sides of his legs were cooling as well. Had he not been alone, he would have been even more embarrassed by his accident. Then again, he wasn't exactly alone, was he?

Had the creature in the tree somehow telepathically sent him that word, that name Arborgork? A few minutes earlier, he would have said such a thing was impossible. Then again, he would have said what he was now looking at; this tree being would have been impossible. Yet here he was, and there it was, and there was that strange word. Maybe he had come up with the word himself. Perhaps he had conjured up that name from deep inside his creative mind.

He knew he did have quite the imagination. Perhaps if he looked away for a moment or closed then reopened his eyes, this thing, this ar-bortion of nature, would be gone. Maybe it would become simply a dead, rotting tree encased in vines. Or perhaps he was dreaming and eventually would wake up slumped on a urine-soaked patio chair. As gross as that sounded, he would prefer it as he could clean up with a quick dip in the pool and then return to his chair. There would be water everywhere, and Lyla would never know the difference when she returned.

Whatever the case, he had to make this horrifying hallucination disappear. He turned away, closed his eyes, and then said a prayer to any deity who might want to get him out of his trouble. He opened his eyes and returned his gaze to the hideous man/tree. It was still as it had been before, and that word was in his mind stronger than ever, "Arborgork." That was when he heard a voice behind him, sounding overwhelmed with disappointment.

"Oh, Ethan . . . I thought you might be the one. I thought you were special. I had really hoped you were. But you weren't, and you failed. You didn't do the one thing I asked of you."

Ethan turned to see Lyla standing behind him, dressed in a long brown hooded robe. She was barefoot, and he could see through the open slit at the front of the robe; she was naked beneath it. He saw tears glistening in her eyes and rolling down her cheeks.

"Lyla?" He said, then fumbled for more words. For a conman such as himself, not developing a way to fast-talk himself out of a situation was unprecedented. Then again, what he was currently experiencing was equally exceptional.

"I told you to stay out of the woods, Ethan. I told you how important trust was to me. Yet here you are, breaking that trust."

"B . . . b . . . but Lyla . . . I . . . I . . ." Ethan stammered, knowing not only that his sweet deal had just gone up in flames but sensing something else. He was in real trouble here. Ethan was half-naked in the middle of a dark forest. He was dealing with a witch of some sort and a . . . what . . . a tree monster, an Arborgork?

"Did you think your charm so overwhelmed me that I wouldn't do my due diligence, Ethan? Did you think I wouldn't have you investigated? Seriously? With all the money involved with my estate. I'm smart, Ethan. And I'm meticulous as well. If I weren't, they would have convicted me of murdering my husband long ago. God knows they tried. But I'm much smarter than that, Ethan. I did do it, you know. I murdered my husband to get his money, but no one will ever be able to prove it. And you won't be telling anyone either."

"But, but Lyla, I love you. You know that."

"I know you love money and have helped yourself to the finances of many women, each time under a different alias. Do you even know your real name anymore? I suspect not. I told you, Ethan, trust is of the utmost importance to me, and apparently, I can't trust you any more than my former lover, who, like you, failed my test."

Ethan's eyes involuntarily shifted over to the tree creature and the name that had popped into his head, Arborgork. He looked back at Lyla and asked, "Is . . . is that . . . that thing . . . is that your . . . your former lover?"

"Yes, but he is only one of the many Arborgorks I have created. Look closer at the other trees."

He suddenly realized two things. The first was that it had been Lyla who had somehow put that strange name, Arborgork, into his mind. The second thing he learned was that Lyla was something much more than she initially appeared to be. She pointed up at the treetops, silently chanting something as the trees spread their branches, allowing shimmering light to shine down to the forest, illuminating as many as ten of the Arborgork creatures.

"Yes, I know, quite a collection I have here. The losers club. The untrustworthy brigade. Each of them failed the test as you did. As such, each of them became Arborgorks for my special collection. As I'm sure by now you've realized, Ethan, you will be joining them very soon."

That was when Ethan turned, deciding it was time for him to beat his feet out of the forest. However, he soon learned he was unable to move those feet. He looked down and saw dozens of vine-like branches had entwined themselves around his ankles and lower legs, grabbing him so tightly he felt like they were crushing his muscles. He tried to scream in pain but found he couldn't utter a sound. He was sure the vines would soon shatter his bones. He could feel a fiery sensation as the small vines pierced his skin, burrowing deep into him. Blood seeped from the wounds and trickled down his legs. The vines absorbed the blood and rapidly multiplied from the nourishment.

Lyla was spinning in a slow circle, chanting some unintelligible incantation. Her eyes were closed, and her hands reached upward as if she were pulling energy from the forest around her. Her hood had fallen, and her long hair flowed wildly in the air as she spun around. The front of her robe had opened, and Ethan could see her beautiful, sweat-soaked naked body at each turn. However, there was no longer anything enticing about that body. The horrible woman wearing that body was destroying his body.

He looked at his legs again and saw the branches had begun to fuse and meld impossibly with his own body. He saw several of the branches that had penetrated his flesh slithering like snakes just under the surface of his skin, making undulating lumps beneath his flesh. Then, miraculously, Ethan realized the incredible pain he was suffering was suddenly gone. He could feel nothing whatsoever.

Paralyzed! he thought and then, with a horrible understanding, *Oh my God, no! The things must have made it to my spine. I can't feel anything.*

That realization was the last conscious thought Ethan Somers ever had. Soon, dozens of thin vine cords made their way up along his spine and into his brain. After that, he had no more thoughts, and his face bore the same idiotic look of complete contentment and passivity every other Arborgork wore. This was still true even as one of the thicker vines made its way up into his throat. It crossed his tongue, over his lips, and eventually out his mouth. The thing slithered and danced in the air for a moment like a snake. Then, it stopped and hardened in place, becoming a solid branch.

Ethan's eyes rolled sightlessly in their sockets. He tried to speak, to cry out, but could do neither. Ethan soon realized that hearing was the only one remaining of all five senses. He could hear the sounds of the forest, the birds singing, a nearby stream flowing, ground animals scurrying amount. Lyla's breathing as she ended her ritual.

He had wanted the estate, the money, and the surrounding forest. In the end, all he managed to get was a permanent place in the woods. The transformation was complete. He had become one with the forest and would join the ranks of the other mindless Arborgorks. Lyla looked at her latest creation with a mixture of satisfaction laced with disappointment. Then she shook her head and headed back home along the path. High above, the tops of the trees returned to their original positions, blocking out the sunlight and returning the forest to darkness.

DREAM IS BUT A LIFE

"All men dream, but not equally. Those who dream by night in the
dusty recesses of their minds wake in the day to find that it was
vanity: but the dreamers of the day are dangerous men, for they
may act on their dreams with open eyes, to make them possible."
—T.E. LAWRENCE

"A dream you dream alone is only a dream.
A dream you dream together is reality."
—JOHN LENNON

"Throw your dreams into space like a kite, and
you do not know what it will bring back, a new life,
a new friend, a new love, a new country."
—ANAIS NIN

"Why do you always have to be such a douchebag, Jim? Come on, just
answer my question."

"You mean your original question or the question as to why I'm
such a douchebag?"

"Never mind, just forget it," Sam said, frustrated. It seemed that
lately, he had become more easily frustrated with everyone.

"Ok. Ok. Don't get your undies in a bunch," Jim replied, "Yes, I
dream, and sometimes I remember my dreams. But most of the time,
I don't remember them, and when I do, they're usually wild and don't

make a ton of sense. Why all the sudden interest in dreams? If you're doing research, I can tell you about a good one I had back when I was thirteen about me and your sister, Jill, if you want."

"Oh wow, this may be a new record for you. I think you managed to go all of fifteen seconds without being a douchebag. But of course, in the end, your inner DB won out as always."

Jim's face contorted into a Popeye the Sailor expression as he said, "I yam what I yam and dats all dat I yam. Yuk, yuk, yuk, yuk, yuk."

Sam shook his head, smiling. No matter how frustrating he might be, his lifelong friend, Jim, always managed to make him laugh. "Ok, ok. But seriously, do you ever have dreams that repeat? You know, like the same places or same people or same situations over and over every night?"

"Uh, honestly? No, I can't say that I do. At least not that I can remember. What's all this about? You sound a bit weird, Sammy 'me boy."

Sam said, "Well, that's because it is weird. My dreams for the past several years have been nothing but weird."

"Did you talk to Amy about them? Your wife's a shrink, after all. Aren't they supposed to know about dreams and crap like that? She should be able to set you straight."

"Yeah, maybe. But these aren't the kind of dreams I can share with my wife. Shrink or not, she wouldn't appreciate hearing them."

"Rutt row, Rorge. Methinks you've had sexy dreams, and Amy ain't the star. Am I right about that?"

Sam hesitated for a moment, then said, "Yeah. But it's more complicated than that. It's like when I dream, I go somewhere else, and I have a completely different life in that other place. The landscape is different, the buildings, the people. Everything is different but me. It's like I exist both here and over there. I have a different wife, a different job, a different home, and different friends. The dream feels every bit as real as me talking to you right now. And when I wake up, I remember every detail of my dream world. When I'm over here and awake, I think of the dream place and feel guilty about being here, you know, with Amy. And when I'm sleeping and with Sandy, my dream wife, I feel guilty about that."

"Ok, let me get this straight. When you're awake, you go to work, come home to your beautiful home, make love to your gorgeous wife, and fall asleep. After you fall asleep, you get to do it all over again with some dream babe named Sandy in a different world. And that bothers you, why?"

"It bothers me because I love my wife and would never cheat on her."

"Which one? Ok, ok, I'm sorry. That was low even by my standards, and I have no standards. But seriously, you're not exactly cheating on Amy, are you? I mean, you're asleep, you're dreaming. We can't control what happens in our dreams. Even if you dream of banging a dozen supermodels, you're still not cheating on your wife."

"I'm telling you, Jim, this is more than just a dream. I mean, I feel like I actually do exist in this other version of my life, and that's what drives me crazy. I love Amy. I'd never cheat on her. Hell, I have no interest in other women at all."

"I sense a big but coming; pun intended."

"Nice, Jim. Very sensitive. When I'm dreaming and with Sandy, it's amazing. But I know what I'm doing is wrong, but I can't stop myself. It feels so right. Then the next morning, I feel like a scumbag. What's been bothering me the most is that I'm having dreams all the time now. They're even starting to trickle into my waking life. You know how sometimes your mind wanders, and you start to daydream? As soon as that happens to me, I'm back in that dream world with Sandy. My dream world seems to be slowly taking over my real world."

"So, you're afraid of what? Do you think you'll go to sleep someday and never wake up? What would that mean? Would your body be like in a coma over here while your mind is living in your dream world? Woah, Dude. That's some pretty heavy crap that brain of yours has cooked up."

"I . . . don't know. Maybe what you suggested could happen. It frightens me, not only because it's happening but because I'm unsure how I feel about it or what to do about it. That is assuming there is anything I can do about it."

"So, it's like you're thinking maybe someday you'll what, stop existing altogether over here and just stay over there . . . in dreamland?

That's weird even for you, Buddy. And what about Amy? Are you just going to vanish someday and leave her wondering where you went off to?"

"That's why I'm telling you. So, if it does happen, you can explain to Amy why it happened."

"Wow, how generous of you. Make me the bearer of bad news. Now, who's being the douchebag?"

"Yeah, I know. But I'm really getting concerned."

Jim was not starting to get angry, "Well, you know what I think? I think you secretly wish that other work was real and that this world was just a dream. Then you could go and live with your dream wife with a clear conscience and forget about Amy and me and everything you have over here. That's what I think, Pal!"

Sam stared at him for a long moment, then said, "Hey, wait a minute. Wait just one damned minute. What did you just say? Maybe I want the other world to be the real world and this one to be the dream. Isn't that what you said?"

"Yeah, that's what I said."

"What if you're right? What if this world is the dream? What if the other world is real?"

"Don't be an idiot, Sam. This world is the only real one. You're real, and I'm real. We've known each other all our lives. We grew up together and graduated together. Hell, I was your best man at your wedding."

Sam looked at Jim strangely and asked, "But we're you? I mean, really? Or did I dream you, and did my sleeping mind make up the whole back story of our friendship to make the dream seem real? Maybe I dreamed Amy, and maybe I'm dreaming my whole life over here."

"Wow! You're losing it, Sammy. You're starting to scare me. Maybe you need to have Amy recommend one of her colleagues to talk with you. You need some serious counseling ASAP. I believe you're cracking up, my friend."

"I knew you were going to say that," Sam said.

"What?"

"What you just said. I knew you were going to say it before you said it. Like I was writing your dialog for you."

"Sam. We've been friends forever. Hell, we can finish each other's sentences. Of course, you knew what I was going to say. Just like I know, you're going to come back with another of your crazy ideas. You need help, Sammy 'me boy."

Just then, they both heard a voice in the distance calling, "Sam, Sam, wake up."

Sam looked at his friend Jim as the man dissolved before his eyes.

Jim looked down at his fading form and said, "Hey. What the Hell. Sam? Sam, what are you doing to m . . ."? But his voice faded away to nothing.

When he awoke, his wife Sandy stood next to his bed and said, "Wake up, sleepyhead. It's Saturday, and we have a busy day ahead of us. I hope you had a good night's sleep."

"I did, Babe. I can't exactly recall the dream I had, but I believe it was one of those that seemed so incredibly realistic."

"Whatever. We have to get moving. Remember we have to go to my company picnic today. We're designated to sit at the table with my boss, Jim, and his wife, Amy, the psychologist. I'd rather not, but it goes with the job, and you know what a douchebag Jim can sometimes be."

INFECTION

The room, if you could call it a room, was not much more than a small, closet-sized space. A large, vertically oriented video screen encompassed the entire front wall from three feet up from the floor to the ceiling. The screen was blank.

J. Carlson Worthington III sat on a comfortable leather chair facing the screen. There was a door behind him, which he had heard someone locking from the outside; he assumed by the same two thuggish characters who had brought him here.

The black cloth bag, which they had placed over his head during transport, was now gone, removed by one of the massive men responsible for bringing him here. He recalled how both men wore black suits, white shirts with black ties, and mirrored sunglasses. They had removed the bag after putting him into the compartment.

His hair was damp with sweat from the stress of his abduction, not to mention the claustrophobic sensation of having the bag over his head. He smelled a sour onion-like reek wafting up from his sodden armpits. The close confines of this cubicle and his foul stench did little to alleviate those claustrophobic feelings.

His captors had been the equivalent of two walking mountains with heads. Each one made three of him in size, if not more, and he suspected they probably farted muscles, judging by the way their arms bulged in the sleeves of their suit jackets.

He hadn't struggled when they "invited" him to come with them for a "very important meeting." Then again, Carlson would have been no match for them. He was in his early seventies, and although fit for his age, he knew and accepted his limitations. This was especially true since having that skiing accident last year. It had seemed to take forever for his broken wrist to heal.

When you add that both man-apes pointed large and intimidating handguns at him, the decision to comply was a no-brainer. As such, he had been cooperative and had not needed to be handcuffed or zip-tied. However, they had insisted he put on the hood so that their meeting location remained a secret.

That had not been a pleasant experience, and he had fought every impulse to pull the hood off, and he could have done so if he chose to since his hands were free. But there had been those two-armed gorillas to deal with as well. There was no rational reason to offer resistance.

Now, in hindsight, Carlson determined his captors had been courteous to him if you discounted the guns they carried. There was also their appearance of being professional leg-breakers. They had been respectful to him, never roughing him up and constantly referring to him as Sir or Mr. Worthington. They had assured him from the outset that they were not kidnapping him but were taking him to a critical secret meeting of other influential individuals. They drew their guns only when he had hesitated initially, and the men insisted on his cooperation. Even then, they were apologetic about having to take such drastic measures.

Now, here he was, locked inside a four-foot square closet resembling a jack-booth in some upscaled adult bookstore. He had known of such places from days gone by, and he had a momentary flashback to his misspent youth. That seemed like a million years ago. Had he ever once been that young and so wild? He supposed he had been once upon a time.

Heavy royal blue material lined the inside of this room from floor to ceiling. Carlson assumed it was some type of soundproofing so that no one would hear him if he chose to shout. Or perhaps it was to guarantee his identity would remain a secret. He had seen no others because of the hood, yet he suspected he was not alone since this was supposed to be an important meeting, after all. Carlson assumed the other guests, apparently as influential as himself, might be waiting in similar booths.

There was a cordial glass on a small, rectangular metal table to his right with a bottle of his favorite Russian vodka next to it, along with an insulated container of ice. Also present was a small tray with a variety of his favorite meats and cheeses, along with some finger sandwiches. Below the sizeable blank video screen was a small shelf with a white button marked "TALK." Also behind it was a small, unlit red lightbulb. Both were directly in front of him.

He pushed the button and asked, "Hello? Hello? Is anybody out there?"

Silence greeted him. He assumed perhaps the talk button was disabled for the time being and that the red light might have something to do with it. He supposed he would have to wait to see.

Suddenly, he heard a digitally altered voice say, "Good evening, ladies and gentlemen. Welcome to this important meeting. As you have been informed, there is a critical reason you have all been summoned here today."

The creepy-sounding disembodied, almost robotic voice seemed to originate through a hidden speaker above Carlson's head somewhere up in the ceiling. He wondered if the "host" of this meeting was watching him and the others through some hidden video camera feed. He suspected he was right about that. After all, it was the sort of thing Carlson would do.

The screen in front of him suddenly sprang to life, and Carlson saw a semi-circular stage cast in darkness and shadows. Near the back end of the stage, a man dressed in a black robe and some nondescript translucent plastic facemask stood behind a bank of computer monitors, conveniently out of view from the guests. A single, lone spotlight shone down from directly above. A microphone on a gooseneck stand was positioned in front of the figure.

Around the circular stage, Carlson saw several other booths that appeared similar to what his own must look like from the outside. However, each one was a different color. Carlson could see purple, orange, green, and yellow booths from his limited view but suspected there would be others.

He saw the hooded figure's hands moving and then heard the voice say, "I will get to the reason for this meeting shortly, but first, I need to cover a few ground rules. Eight of you are stationed in eight colored booths: red, yellow, blue, green, orange, violet, white and black. You may collectively be of both sexes as well as various races. Or you might not be. Only I know if that statement is true or false. And to be honest, the less you know about each other, the better off you will be.

"I should point out here that discovering the identity of any of your counterparts at this meeting could prove fatal to you. I can't stress enough that I am not exaggerating when I use the word fatal, either. That being said. I will be referring to you generically as Mister for your safety and anonymity. For example, Mr. Red, Mr. Green, and Mr. Blue match the booths in which you now sit.

Carlson thought, *Hey, he stole that color name idea from that Quentin Tarantino movie. What was that called?* Then the name came to him: *Reservoir Dogs.* He remembered the actor Steve Buscemi's character complaining about being Mr. Pink. However, it was much more entertaining in the movie than in real life.

The voice continued, "Again, please forgive all the cloak and dagger. However, it is necessary to protect your identities from each other and eventually from the rest of the world. Today, what you will learn will put you in a particularly vulnerable position regarding the general public, or those I prefer to call the great unwashed. In other words, lynching following a tar and feathering by the masses would be a picnic compared to what people might do to you. Now, let's discuss your participation in this meeting.

"You will not be able to be heard until a time at which I want you to be heard. You'll notice a white button labeled 'Talk' in front of you. Do NOT press it at this time. I repeat, DO NOT PRESS IT at this time. Later, when our discussion begins, you may press the white button to indicate you want to speak. It will register here on my monitors, and I will decide whether to have you speak. When I want you to speak, a red light will illuminate in your cubicle, indicating it is your turn to begin speaking. Your voices, of course, will be altered as mine has been. But I repeat yet again: DO NOT press the white button at this time.

Suddenly, the host's panel lit up with requests to speak from every one of the captors. All the participants had pressed their buttons, each wanting to get their opinions heard first to one-up the competition. That was the problem with the self-important, rich and powerful. In any given situation, they feel their opinions are not only the most important and that no one else's opinion matters but that the rest of the world is on pins and needles, waiting to embrace their incredible insights. The masked moderator looked at the eight flashing lights on his panel and shook his head in frustrated resignation. He had anticipated this reaction but had hoped he would be wrong.

Then he spoke, "Did I not just give you all specific instructions three separate times NOT to press the white button? Yet every one of you disobeyed me and pressed your buttons anyway. I'm not in the least bit surprised. I've dealt with your sort of people many times before. I probably would have been more shocked if you didn't act like the obnoxious, self-important morons you all are. However, this is my meeting, and that means you MUST follow my rules."

The mysterious host reached up and began slowly turning a dial in his control panel. As Carlson sat in his cubicle, he began to feel a tingling sensation going through his body. It rapidly grew stronger until he realized what he felt was an ever-increasing electric shock. His teeth clamped down tightly. Had his tongue not been out of the way, indeed, he might have bitten it off. His muscles tensed as the humming pain surged through him. His body went rigid as his buttocks involuntarily lifted out of the seat. His heart seemed to skip a beat, perhaps stop in his chest. He was sure he was going to die. Then, in an instant, the sensation stopped, and he fell back to his seat soaked in a cold sweat.

"What the Hell was that?" Carlson shouted.

A moment later, he once again heard the calm voice of their host coming over the speaker. "There now, isn't that better? Please allow me to reiterate my previous statement. I have specific rules when I am conducting my meetings. Compliance with those rules is mandatory, and those who follow my rules will leave here at the end of the meeting, alive and unharmed. Those who fail to comply will not fare so well."

The microphone went silent, and just before the screen in front of him went black, Carlson saw another man in a similar hooded coat and semi-clear plastic face mask approach the host from somewhere off to the side. Then Carlson sat for what seemed like an hour but was only a few minutes. Once again, the screen came to life, and the second man was gone. The host sat behind his console, appearing to be thinking about what to say. Then his computer-enhanced voice returned.

"It appears Mr. Black is no longer with us. His heart was unable to handle my little demonstration. Oh well, someone had to be the first. Hopefully, he will be the last. However, I am an amateur student of human behavior, and if I'm correct, which I usually am, I'm quite certain there will be more." Then, the man hesitated to give the meeting attendees a chance to absorb what he had just said.

Carlson sat staring at the screen dumbfounded. Dead? One of the eight, Mr. Black, was killed? How could that be? Then again, he had felt the force of that electroshock. Hadn't he wondered, even just for a moment, if he might not survive? Of course, he had. He reached over to the bottle of vodka and, adding a few ice cubes to the glass, poured in a significant amount of the clear liquid. He managed to get his hands to stop trembling long enough to take a healthy sip. Soon, he was feeling a bit better. What the Hell was all this about?

The host spoke again, "If I may make this situation as straightforward as possible for you, it's like this. Out there, in what you may think of as the real world, you people are all significant movers, shakers, and high financial decision-makers. However, what you don't realize is there are powers at work in the world that make your assumed influence seem minuscule by comparison. This meeting is being held at the request of an organization comprised of those influential individuals. I have been chosen to act as their representative. I have been given the authority to do whatever I feel is necessary. So, for the record, here I am in charge. I make the rules, and I choose the punishment for violations of those rules.

"We have not brought you all here to render your opinions. You are here to listen, to learn, to side with us eventually, and by doing so, to survive. You are not here because we like or respect any of you. You are here because your wealth and the power you wield outside these walls motivate us to make you our partners. In essence, you are somewhat of a necessary evil. This is not to suggest we couldn't continue without you, and will if necessary. However, our goals will be more easily attainable with your cooperation.

"Now for some background. I must beg your patient indulgence as this explanation might go on for quite a bit. I'll do my best to keep it as short as possible, although I do tend to ramble on. As you know, there is a problem in our country regarding our social security system. Some of the blame can go to mismanagement by our elected officials. Since they are no more than puppets whose strings we pull, I suppose that portion of the responsibility falls upon my organization. However, a more significant part of the problem is that the greatest percentage of our population is getting older. The so-called baby boomers, a group of which most of us are members, are putting a burden on the system, which it can't possibly handle.

"We do acknowledge that any person collecting social security has been contributing to the system involuntarily for all of their working years. As such, when they start collecting their Social Security checks, they will be doing nothing more than reacquiring their own money. But, specific considerations were missed when social security was put into place. The founders of this program hadn't anticipated how much the average life span would increase. Nor did they realize how many people would continue to collect paychecks while collecting social security, double-dipping, if you will. People whose jobs offer decent medical benefits keep working, often specifically to take advantage of that medical coverage. This means older, less energetic workers take jobs away from younger, more vital, more productive workers.

"In addition, these people are putting an enormous strain on our health care system. They are responsible for more than seventy-five percent of hospital resources, causing less attentive care for younger, more essential people. They also tend to be at the top of the pay scale instead of a less expensive young person. Yes, as I said, I realize many of you in this meeting fall into the category of baby boomers or older people. However, you have all done exceptionally well for yourselves and are not contributing to the burden. That is another reason why you are here.

"As you may recall, a few years back, the world was essentially locked down because of the spread of COVID-19 Coronavirus. Whether the virus was natural or man-made and whether its origin was deliberate or accidental is irrelevant for our purposes. What is relevant is that the most significant number of deaths from the virus was among the elderly. The disease ripped through rest homes like a forest fire, killing thousands.

"This gave us an idea. Suppose we were to release a similar virus in our country and make sure the focus of that release was on the places where people of social security age were found, such as retirement communities, fifty-five-plus developments, rest homes, and so on. What impact would that have on the social security system? We ran the numbers, did the models and simulations, and found that we could wipe out almost ninety percent of people over 65 within four months. Ladies and gentlemen, we could save the social security system, reduce the burden on our healthcare system and strengthen the economy for our younger residents as they inherit their parents and grandparents' substantial estates.

"Think about it. Social security was put in place to help people survive in their twilight years. When we established social security, no one had any idea that the boomer generation would be so financially successful. Not only has this generation risen to a higher financial level than previous generations, but for the first time in this country's history, they are more financially established than the younger generation coming up behind them. And still, these people dare to receive social security checks on top of that income. Most of them don't even need money.

"So, what are we going to do about it? As I speak, 10,000 young people we've trained to be our undercover agents have been infected with a new strain of virus very similar to the old COVID-19, only much more lethal. These well-paid individuals were not only chosen for being young and potentially strong enough to be able to survive the virus but also because each of them works in a position, which brings them in direct contact with the elderly."

Suddenly, the screen in front of Carlson was filled with a graph that had an ever-increasing line starting at the lower-left angle and climbing upward to the right. He had seen enough diagrams in his long life to know this sort of rapid climb was not good. It climbed far too steeply in far too short a period.

"As you can see, based on our models, this virus will spread quickly and, within a few months, will do the work we designed it to do. Then, if handled properly, the virus will run its course and then die out. This is where you people become essential. This is where you can help our cause. As back in the COVID-19 days, we need people to spearhead our campaign to rally the people to join the fight and work together for the good of our nation.

"Your people and your various corporations will all begin preparing for a media frenzy of campaigns dedicated to uniting the people against this dreaded virus. We'll claim it originated in China. It didn't, of course, but that's what we want people to think, and of course, they'll believe us. We'll instruct the governors of all states to initiate a national shutdown as they did with COVID-19. However, it won't be until we have infected many elderly people.

"As I'm sure you recall, COVID-19 was successfully eradicated not only by experimental drugs and vaccines but by the unprecedented shutting down of non-essential businesses and the implementation of social distancing. None of these measures were well received, and it essentially wiped out many small businesses in the country. However, as people invested in large corporations, you all saw financial windfalls. Plus, with so many small businesses failing, it paved the way for further expansion of your various significant corporate interests. Some think of this as the homogenization of America, while we prefer to think of it as standardization.

"I think I've gone on for far too long. Again, I want to thank you all for your patience. I'll entertain questions currently. I'm certain you have many. You may press your white buttons to speak. When I address you, and you see the red light illuminate, you may begin speaking."

At first, Carlson was too shocked to speak. Then he realized he had something to ask after all. He pressed the white button, momentarily expecting to receive another electric shock, which fortunately never came. After a moment, the red light illuminated, and the voice said, "Mr. Blue, you may speak."

Carlson hesitated for a beat, weighing his words carefully, then said, "If I understand you correctly, you are asking all of us here to become part of what is essentially a genocidal plot, a plan to kill millions of older Americans. Is that correct?"

"Thank you for the question, Mr. Blue, although I take umbrage with your use of the concept of genocide. For millennia, it has been the way of nature to weed out the old, the weak, and the sick to make way for the young and the strong for the herd's survival. We simply are helping Mother Earth by speeding up the process. We are not doing this with evil intentions. It has been carefully debated and planned. Think of it as a lion stalking a herd of wildebeests. The lion systematically chooses the oldest and weakest of the animals. I hope that clears things up for you. Oh, I see we have another question. Mr. Orange wants to speak. Go ahead, Mr. Orange."

Carlson heard a voice come over the speaker, "What about us? What about our families? What if they catch this virus?"

"Well, Mr. Orange. That's another reason you're here. In exchange for your continued cooperation, you will have a several-week head start to get your children and grandchildren somewhere safe, likely somewhere off U.S. soil for a while. Maybe Europe or perhaps Hawaii would be a good place. It would be best if you got them away from the country since, eventually, this virus will spread outside of the elderly population no matter what we do to try to contain it. There will be some casualties among the under-fifty population, but our models suggest no more than fifty thousand or so. It's an acceptable risk compared to the millions of old folks going down. Mr. Violet, I see you have a question."

A moment later, a mechanized voice shouted, "You and your group must be mad! We cannot stand by and allow you to exterminate an entire generation of Americans systematically. I won't stand for it. I demand you release us all immediately. Perhaps it's still not too late to stop this . . . this . . . this insanity!"

Carlson had no idea who Mr. Violet was or if he was a man at all. But whoever he was, Carlson agreed with him 100 percent. He was about to press his white button and ask to speak again when he heard their host say, "Those are pretty strong feelings you're expressing there, Mr. Violet. Maybe you need to rethink your position. Isn't that right, Mr. Black?"

Mr. Black? Carlson thought to himself. *That's impossible; Mr. Black is dead. He had a heart attack no more than a few minutes ago.*

A voice came from the speaker, "Yes. I think Mr. Violet may have spoken in haste. Perhaps he needs a few minutes to reconsider. Or perhaps you can explain a bit more about their situation. For example, how I, Mr. Black, can be speaking when Mr. Black was, no more, deceased, passed away, gone over to the other side, el dead-a-mundo."

"Great idea, Mr. Black. Or should I say Mr. Black two-point-o?" the voice said, "OK, everyone. Just in case you haven't been paying attention, Mr. Black, the original Mr. Black, died several minutes ago, and we removed his still-cooling corpse from this meeting. His body will be placed behind his desk in his office, where it will be found tomorrow by one of the many workers he forces to arrive early in the morning and stay until late in the evening. But enough of that. Out with the old and in with the new. Enter replacement, Mr. Black. He was once an employee of the now-deceased original Mr. Black. But unlike his predecessor, this Mr. Black is much more in tune with the importance of our mission."

Carlson realized the seriousness of his situation. If they could replace Mr. Black with one of his underlings in a matter of minutes, then the same thing could happen to any one of the so-called essential people in this room. Obviously, this organization had recruited one or more people from each of their corporations and had paid them sufficiently so they would be willing to take the top spot in the event Carlson or the others threatened to go against them.

The host's voice once again came over the speaker, saying, "I'm sure by now most of you, at least the smartest among you, have figured out the game plan here. But let me reiterate once more. We want you all to buy into our strategy. You are all recognizable faces representing your many corporations. That is a valuable commodity to have you support our strategy. However, and I can't stress this enough if you try to stand in our way or to go against us, we have others waiting in the wings to take each of your places if needed."

Carlson began to wonder which of his dozen or so next in commands would be willing to sell him out for the chance to take his place. Maybe Johnson, the CEO of his Atlanta manufacturing division. Or perhaps it was Alexander, the CFO in finance. Carlson suddenly realized how tenuous his grip was on his multi-billion-dollar empire. Two days ago, he never would have had such thoughts, but two days ago seemed like a lifetime ago. He suddenly understood the expression, "Ignorance is bliss." He had been ignorant of his vulnerabilities. Now, after being reminded of his real place in the actual pecking order of life, he knew better.

The voice came over the speaker once again, "So, Mr. Violet, earlier, you said you could not allow us to exterminate an entire generation of Americans systematically. If I remember correctly, you said you would not stand for it. I'd like to think that after that last bit of enlightening information, perhaps you might have seen the error of your ways. Can I make that assumption?"

The speaker was silent for a few long moments, then the computerized voice of Mr. Violet reluctantly said, "Um, uh well . . . why yes . . . Now that I've had some time, you know, some time to . . . to think about it . . . yes, the plan sounds quite rational to me. Yes, quite a good idea indeed."

The host replied, "Excellent, Mr. Violet; great to see you're on board. The good Lord loves a team player."

Carlson thought, *Of course, he's onboard. You threatened to kill the man, for God's sake.* But, of course, Carlson said nothing.

Then the host said, "But here's the problem, Mr. Violet. I don't believe you have signed up for this; drank the Kool-Aid, so to speak. Sure, you said the right words, and maybe someone who was less astute than me might buy what you're selling. Lord knows you've made billions doing just that. But the truth is, I don't believe you for an instant. What I do believe is as soon as this meeting is over and you return to your regular duties, you're going to do everything in your power to try to stop us. Isn't that right, Mr. Violet?"

Mr. Violet spoke up, "Nnnnno . . . no, not at all. I'm on your side; I'm a team player. I'm in complete agreement. Please, please believe me."

The mysterious host made the sound of a buzzer saying, Aaaaatttt! Wrong answer. Time for a teachable moment. I'll keep your microphone on active so all our students can learn."

At first, Carlson heard Mr. Violet's continued pleas for mercy. Then he heard a low rumbling buzz they each recognized as the slow increase of electric current. Mr. Violet began to scream as the buzzing grew louder. Soon, his screams became ear-piercing howls of agony. Then the buzzing stopped, and the collective group heard a thudding sound as Mr. Violet's corpse fell to the floor.

Carlson was about to shout out against this maniac when another voice came over his speaker, "You rotten bastards! You'll never get away with this! I swear I'll see every one of you on death row for this."

That was when Carlson realized all their microphones were active. He looked down and saw the illuminated red light on the console in front of him. That meant the host deliberately activated their microphones so he could capture their reactions to the sounds of the execution of Mr. Violet.

"Mr. Green. You, too, seem to harbor negative sentiments toward my organization and me. Perhaps you would like to share them further with each of our guests."

The view of the screen in front of Carlson Suddenly changed. He correctly assumed the screens in front of the rest of the captives changed as well. Gone was the hooded man in the translucent face mask, having been replaced by a view of a different man, a terrified man sitting inside a booth lined with bright green carpeting. He was looking up toward the top of the booth. His screen was blank, but his red "talk" button was illuminated.

Carlson recognized the man immediately. It was H. Jonathan Waldman, president and CEO of one the country's largest conglomerates, one perhaps one and a half times as large as his own. He had managed to take an almost defunct automobile giant and bring it back from ruin to glory. He had been featured in many television commercials and wrote an autobiography, which had become a best seller.

Waldman began shouting, "No, please, listen to me, everyone. We have to stop these people. They're insane, don't you see that? I'm H. Jonathan Waldman, for God's sake. I don't know who you all are, but I suspect we've all done business together. I may have broken bread with a few of you. We must stop this madness now. We have to . . . ahhhhhh!"

Waldman, aka Mr. Green, was screaming and thrashing spasmodically within the confines of his booth. Arcs of blue lightning seemed to fly in from the floor and walls and course through his twitching, gyrating body. Smoke began climbing up from the now-smoldering billionaire for a few seconds. Soon, the spasming stopped, and the man collapsed in the chair resembling an unstuffed rag doll, albeit one that was smoking.

"It appears Mr. Green is no longer with us. His replacement is standing by. Unfortunately, this body will be found in the burned-out remains of a fire in an abandoned row home in a section of the city populated by drug addicts and hookers. They will use dental records to identify him. Because of his notoriety, it will all be covered up sufficiently. But that fabrication will be the responsibility of his widow and children. She won't be happy to discover her beloved husband frequented such places. He didn't, of course, but we'll make it look like he did, and despite the best efforts of his widow, we'll make sure the press learns of his 'indiscretions.' I know they'll feast on a morsel as juicy as this one.

"One other thing, I'm sure most, if not almost all, of you recognized Mr. Green. For those of you who did not, you got to hear him state that his name was H. Jonathan Waldman. Even if you didn't know the face, I'm sure you recognize the name. It's not very easy to be one of the richest men in the country without someone recognizing your name. You may remember how I said earlier it would be bad for any of you to see or identify each other. That remains true. Nonetheless, I decided to make sure each of you saw him and knew his name.

"I also had you witness his death for several reasons. For one thing, you are now all complicit in his death. You may not have participated in his death or been responsible for causing his demise; that bit of creativity was all my own. However, you did witness his electrocution. Although there was nothing any of you could do to help him, each of you witnessed it. The thing is, no matter how much you might want to tell someone about it, if you are fortunate to get out of this meeting alive, you won't. Each of you will remain silent, and this is the reason why. If you leave here and even the slightest rumor of what happened here gets out, each of you will suffer a fatal accident. At least, that's how it will look to the authorities. Think about what just happened to Mr. Green. He got off easy. You will not. And by the way, if even one of you screws up, you all die. And that death will not be pleasant.

"What makes it all even more interesting is you each have no idea who the other is. You are all tied by the death of Mr. Green, but you can't even accidentally discuss it with each other because you haven't a clue who any of you are. Quite ingenious, wouldn't you agree?"

"I'm Carlson Worthington!" Carlson shouted, assuming his microphone was still active.

The voice chuckled and said, "Nice try, Mr. Blue. However, I have muted all your microphones. I should point out that it's lucky for you and the occupants of the other booths as well. You might have inadvertently caused the death of your companions by making them aware of you. You seem to forget I control all aspects of this meeting. I choose who you learn about and who you don't. I choose who lives and who dies. I decide who gets punished and how severely. Oh, and for your information, from this point forward, if one of you does something worthy of punishment, you all will get the same punishment. That is, all but our loyal replacements."

The mysterious figure reached up and once again began to turn the knob slowly as he had done before. Once again, Carlson felt the electric current flowing through his body. As before, it happened so quickly that he was unable to stand up.

"He's going to kill me this time," Carlson was certain. He believed his captors had no intention of letting any of them leave alive. It was all some sick game they had found themselves in the middle of, and death might be the only escape.

The current stopped, and Carlson dropped into his chair, smelling the sour stench of his sweat . . . and something else.

Oh God, no, not that! Please, no, Carlson thought upon realizing his bladder had let loose, and he was sitting in a puddle of his urine. *What if he turns on the juice again? Will I get electrocuted? Is that what happened to Mr. Black?*

"Oh my, Mr. Blue," The voice said, "It appears we've had a bit of an accident. Not to worry, everyone, nobody else died. Mr. Blue just . . . um . . . shall we say . . . pissed himself. I think this would be a good time for a break. Take a drink, folks. Eat a few mini sandwiches. That is, everyone but Mr. Blue."

Everyone but me? Carlson thought a second before the door behind him flew open, and four strong arms reached in. Two of the arms pulled the hood back over his head while two other arms lifted him out of his seat and dropped him onto the carpet outside his compartment. Then, chaos became the order of the day. While someone held him down, some other person or persons unbuckled his belt and quickly pulled down both his slacks and sodden undershorts.

Oh my God, sweet Jesus, they're going to rape me. This was the first thought which ran through Carlson's mind. That would be his punishment for shouting his name. Oh yes, he was going to pay for that outburst. It would probably be one of the two man-apes who brought him here. He could only hope they weren't as big and muscular between their legs as the rest of them were. If they were, then he was in for some significant pain.

To Carson's surprise, someone threw a wet cloth on his upper legs and said, "Clean yourself up. Don't touch the hood."

Carlson went to work cleaning himself as instructed, then someone tossed a dry towel to him, and he dried himself off as well. Next, he felt a pair of sweatpants land on his legs. He bent and slipped them on.

I guess I'm going commando, he thought, amazed that he could still find any part of this day even slightly humorous.

Before he had time to think about it, two strong arms lifted him roughly, and he felt a sharp pricking in his right arm. *They injected me with something,* he thought.

Next, he found himself back inside the blue booth. Someone had cleaned and dried his chair, but he could tell by the urine stench in the close confines of the booth they had done nothing with the floor.

The voice said, "Welcome back, Mr. Blue. I trust all is satisfactory. As you may have noticed, we take care of the people who matter to us, and all of you remaining are important to our cause. Mr. Blue, your cohorts have also returned from a much-needed break. You should be happy these people don't know your real identity, Mr. Blue. As I said, when one of you is punished, you all are punished. When you were shocked, all of your cohorts were shocked as well. After what you just put them through, I would guess you would have few, if any, friends among this group.

"So now that we are all back and ready to go, do we have any more questions or open items to discuss before we move on? Let's start with Mr. Blue. Any questions, Mr. Blue?"

Carlson looked down and saw his red light glowed. That meant he had better speak out now, or else he would lose his opportunity to do so. He decided the only chance he had of getting out of this mess alive was to sound convincing. He would have to make them believe he had seen the light. But he couldn't try too hard, or he was sure they would see through his deceit.

He said, "No questions. It's clear this is a done deal, and there is nothing any of us can do but protect our loved ones and support your decision by doing as you ask."

"Excellent, Mr. Blue. Glad to see you decided to come on board. I could sense the slight frustration in your voice, and that is perfectly understandable. This was not an easy decision to make, and I would be shocked if you didn't feel at least a bit apprehensive. However, I am glad to find you have come to see things our way. How about the rest of you?"

Then, one by one, the host went from booth to booth, asking each remaining person to pledge their fidelity to the cause. And each of them did. To Carlson's relief, after a few moments, the back of his booth was pulled open again. Someone put the hood over his head for the third time. Two strong arms led him to a waiting vehicle, and after what seemed like several hours, he was unceremoniously dropped onto his driveway.

He felt someone leaning close to him, saying, "Wait five minutes after you hear our car leave before removing the hood . . . say nothing of this experience to anyone ever . . . we will be watching. We will be in touch to let you know when we need your assistance and what you must do for us. When we do, you will answer the call and do what must be done; whatever must be done."

Carlson asked, "Wha . . . what if it's something I can't do or don't feel comfortable doing? I don't want to do anything to hurt anyone or do anything illegal."

The voice said, "That ship has sailed, Mr. Worthington. You are already up to your neck in illegality, and millions will die because of what you are now part of. So, no matter what we ask of you, you will obey. If we ask you to assassinate the president, you will do it. Now, perhaps you should go and take care of your beautiful wife, Julie, and that gorgeous young teenage daughter of yours. What's her name? Oh yeah, Cindy. I could only imagine what horrible fate might befall poor innocent Cindy if you failed to meet your obligations, Mr. Worthington."

Carlson sat in the driveway, smelling the night breeze through his hood and wishing he had spoken up, wishing he had refused to help these madmen. Had he done so, he would be as dead as the others who didn't survive the meeting. But at least it was over for them. For J. Carlson Worthington III, the horror was just beginning.

Right before he heard the car door slam, one of the men said, "Oh, and by the way, your wife and daughter will have a story to tell you about an unpleasant abduction they had in your absence. Not to worry, they were not . . . um . . . violated in any way. However, they were injected with the same nanorobot we injected into you and your other meeting attendees. Suppose you ever do anything to make us feel you are not supporting our plan. In that case, we will activate those nanorobots remotely, and each of you will suffer an immediate and highly agonizing brain hemorrhage followed by death. Have a nice day, Mr. Worthington.

DEATH THROWS THE DART

"I don't throw darts, I bet on a sure thing."
—GORDON GEKKO, *WALL STREET*

"If you don't mind my saying so, you look like a man with far too many troubles," the bartender said to the white-haired man sitting alone at the bar.

It was a slow night, to say the least. Only one other couple was at a table near the front end of the establishment, and a server was handling them. However, that couple wouldn't keep the bartender busy since they had been nursing the same drinks for the past hour. If a bar had to rely on people like that, it would go under in a month. But that was ok since the dismal-looking sole patron at the bar was his point of focus anyway.

The man was on his fourth vodka and Sprite, and he didn't seem ready to slow down any time soon. He lifted his head away from the glass, which he appeared to be attempting to stare a hole in, and his bloodshot eyes met the bartender's curious gaze.

"I asked if everything was ok," the bartender repeated.

"Yeah . . . yeah, I'm fine, or I should say I will be fine as soon as I come to terms with what's happening."

The bartender asked, "Sorry, pal, I'm not quite following you. What's the problem?"

The man appeared to be in his late sixties or early seventies. He had a surprisingly full head of snow-white hair with thick, matching eyebrows. His skin was aged but not the flesh of a lifetime drinker. No, this man was not accustomed to spending time in bars or drinking, especially drinking at his current rate. He sighed deeply, then replied.

"It's just . . . I don't know . . . it just seems like everyone around me is either sick, dying, or dead. I just lost a close friend today . . . and another one, two weeks ago. Several other people I know are dealing with terminal illnesses. It seems every time I turn around, someone else is gone."

The bartender replied, "Yeah, it's always tough losing friends. I've lost a few this year myself. If you don't mind my saying so, you appear to be at that age when this sort of thing is something you should expect."

The man shook his head as he returned to staring at his glass, "I know I am, and I do understand the uncertainty of longevity for people in my age bracket. However, it's more than that. It's something I feel is potentially much worse, something hard to explain."

"Feel free to try, my friend. Ain't nobody here but you and me, and I ain't got nothing but time," the bartender replied.

"Well, it's kinda like something that happened to me back when I was in my twenties. You see, I was working for this company. We occupied three floors of a four-story office building. Lots of employees, you know?"

The bartender nodded his head, silently encouraging the man to continue.

"As it happened, business took a downturn, and one rainy Friday, the company had to fire a bunch of people. Those of us who survived the slaughter referred to it as Black Friday. Anyway, there were so many people getting nailed that day, the company set up a temporary unemployment office on the unused fourth floor, so anybody getting canned could sign up for unemployment right away."

"Sounds pretty efficient," the bartender said.

"That it was as efficient as a Nazi gas chamber. But that made it all the more terrifying. You see, back then, we didn't have computers or those mazes of cubicles that offices have today. We had open floor plans with desks lined up in a grid pattern, as you see in those old black-and-white TV shows and movies. You know what I mean?"

The bartender nodded, "Yep, I remember."

"Well, all around the open floor of desks, the bosses had their glassed-in offices. Starting promptly at 9:00, as we all sat rigidly at our desks, pretending to be working, a boss would stroll from his office looking depressed, approach one of the workers, tap him on the shoulder, and say something to him. Then they would both walk to the elevator, go up to the fourth floor, and the employee would never be seen again."

"Sounds rough," the bartender replied.

"It was. But the hardest part was waiting and not knowing if you would be next. I remember seeing the elevator doors slowly opening time after time and the bosses walking over and tapping another guy on the shoulder, then back into the elevator they went. I remember thinking, is my time up? Would they come for me?"

The bartender gave the man a look of understanding and said, "Man, that must have been traumatic for you, especially since it still bothers you so many years later."

"It does, but only because that's how I feel again. I feel like I'm sitting at my desk, but now it's death coming out of that elevator. He's walking around tapping my friends on the shoulder one by one and taking them into the elevator. The worst part is I know, sooner or later, I'm going to feel his icy fingers tapping me on the shoulder, and it will be my turn. See what I mean?"

"Yeah, I believe I do. That's a good analogy, although pretty scary. I always felt death was much more random than that."

"How so?" The man asked.

The bartender replied, "Well, for me, when I think of death, I imagine one of those carnival midway games. You know, the one where there are several hundred balloons of different colors pinned to a wooden backboard, and each color is associated with a specific shelf of prizes. When you throw a dart and pop a balloon, you get to pick a prize from the shelf associated with that color."

"Ok . . ." the man said, sounding like he might not be following the analogy.

"Well, the way I see it is like this. You're the balloons, and death is the guy with the darts. When he's ready to collect another soul, he throws a dart at the cluster of balloons and randomly pops one. No plan, no purpose; it's all random. See, in your analogy, the situation was based on a plan. The company knew who they were getting rid of even though the employees didn't until it happened. The same thing was true with death. But in mine, even death didn't know or didn't care for that matter. He just threw the dart and let it hit wherever it hit."

"Random?"

"Yep, completely random. That's why it all seems so unfair: how one man can live into his nineties while another dies in his twenties. Or why a small child can be terminally ill while another is perfectly healthy. It's all random with no plan and no purpose."

"Somehow, that seems even worse, even more terrifying. There's something about the lack of a plan or purpose of death that makes me feel even less significant than I did before. If this was your attempt to make me feel better, you failed miserably, my friend."

"That wasn't my intention, and I'm sorry if I bummed you out. I just wanted to explain how I see things. Life is random. So is death. For example, you didn't plan on coming in here tonight. I'll wager you've never been in here before. Am I right?"

"Yeah, you're right."

"And we've never met before, right?"

"Right."

"Yet here we are, discussing life and death. You with your analogy, and I with mine. Which one is more accurate? Does it even matter? I suspect not. Life is life, and death is death. Life is what we make it, and death is what it will be."

"That pretty deep . . ."

"For a bartender?"

"Sorry, I meant no offense," the man said.

"None taken, Jim."

The man was taken aback for a moment, "Say, I don't believe I told you my name."

"You didn't. But I saw it back there, among the others."

"What?" Jim said with surprise as he turned to look in the direction the bartender was pointing.

A wooden wall covered with small multicolored inflated balloons was at the room's far end. Jim could see the wall underneath was scarred with thousands of tiny holes like those made by years of darts piercing its surface. Each balloon had a different name written on its skin. Jim could read the outside of a red balloon slightly larger than the others from where he sat. It read, James Thomas Arner . . . his name.

Jim turned back and shouted, "Hey, what's going on here . . ." The bartender was gone. He looked around, and the couple was gone, as was the server. He looked back at the wall of balloons and saw a shadowed form standing in front of the wall. It was tall and clad in a black hooded robe. It held a bright red dart with a shiny bronze tip in its skeletal fingers.

As the figure raised its arm to throw the dart, it turned and gave Jim a hideous smile through tombstone teeth. Jim knew which balloon it would hit.

HARBINGER OF DEATH

Kerry squinted as he tried to find his way through the mist and fog covering the roadway before him. He recalled how he had always hated this two-lane farm road, even under the best of conditions. He had forgotten about that since it had been years since he had come this way. His cousin, Jim, had called Kerry to say his father, Kerry's Uncle Fred, was dying. Fred wanted to see his nephew one last time before he passed.

Kerry found it strange that his uncle had made such a request. True, he had been close to his uncle in his younger years, but the hectic business of day-to-day living had left little time for them to see each other during the past decade or more. Now, time had caught up with them, and the best Kerry could hope for was to say one final goodbye to the man he had once thought of as a second father. His father had died when Kerry was a teenager, and his Uncle Fred had stepped in to nurture him and guide him into manhood. Perhaps he would have time to let the man know what a positive influence he had been and thank him properly for all he had done.

As his car rounded a long bend, Kerry saw something in the mist ahead. He turned the wheel sharply to the left, nearly striking what appeared to be a man dressed in a dark hooded sweatshirt, bending down to pick something up from the side of the highway.

As he passed treacherously close to the hunched figure, Kerry slammed his fist onto his horn and screamed, "Idiot. What the hell are you doing picking up road garbage in this weather!"

But the man didn't seem to hear either his honking horn or his shouts of frustration. In his rearview mirror, Kerry could see the man continuing to bend over as he walked, picking up various objects as if nothing had happened. He drove on for a mile or so, then pulled over. Kerry took a series of deep, calming breaths to control his now trembling hands. He kept looking in his rearview mirror to see if the man was catching up to him, but the mirror remained empty. After about ten minutes or so, he felt relaxed enough to go on.

Oh my God, I could have killed that man, he thought to himself, *If I had, I would have had to live with that for the rest of my life, all because that moron was stupid enough to be out picking up garbage.*

As Kerry pulled into the driveway of his uncle's farm and approached his two-story brick home, he saw his cousin Jim waiting in the doorway to greet him. He pulled his car over and got out to meet his cousin. Kerry could see something was very wrong by the evident sorrow on the man's face. He hugged his cousin and said, "Sorry, Bro. It's been too long since I was here. That's my fault. I wish my visit were under better circumstances."

"He's gone, Kerry," Jim said, not wasting time on formalities, "He passed no more than a few minutes ago."

Kerry shook his head in frustration, "Oh God no. I'm so sorry, Jim. I so wanted to say goodbye to Uncle Fred. I really wanted to thank him for being there for me after Dad died. I would have been here earlier, but I nearly hit some idiot walking along the road in the fog. It shook me up so badly I had to pull over for a bit. I couldn't believe that moron was just walking around picking up crap off the highway in the middle of a fog bank. That's like asking to be run over."

Despite his obvious grief, Jim got an odd look on his face and said, "It wouldn't have mattered if you had hit him, Kerry, because he wasn't really there."

In confusion, Kerry looked at his cousin and said, "What are you talking about? If I had hit him, he would have been road pizza."

"Come on in, and I'll tell you all about it. But first, I'll take you back to see Dad if you would like. I called the funeral home, and they should be here within the hour."

"Um . . . ok," Kerry said reluctantly. He was never fond of looking at dead people and hardly ever attended funerals for that reason. He had never seen a dead body outside of a funeral parlor either, so the idea of looking at one in a bed in someone's home didn't sit so well with him. But he realized he would have to man up and do what he needed to do.

When they got to the doorway of his uncle's bedroom, Kerry felt a bit light-headed as tiny prickles of goose flesh seemed to pass all through his body. He forced himself to ignore the feelings of apprehension and follow his cousin into the death room. Kerry saw his Uncle Fred lying in bed with covers around his chest and his arms draped down on top of them. He looked peaceful to Kerry, much like bodies he had seen in coffins. This made him feel somewhat better.

"Dad loved you, Kerry. I'm sure he thought of you as his second son," Jim said.

Kerry didn't know what to say. He was never prone to showing or expressing his emotions, especially those of love and affection. "Um . . . he was a great man, Jim. I feel bad that I have been away for so long. He did a lot for me growing up. I wanted to tell him how much I appreciated that before he . . ."

Jim said, "I'm sure he knew, Kerry. He spoke about you often. He understood how things were, how a busy working life always seemed to get in the way of living. He only learned to appreciate that after he retired. Come on, let's go out in the living room and sit down. I have something to tell you about your mysterious stranger on the highway. Would you like a beer?"

"I hate to ask, but do you have anything stronger? After the morning I've had, a nice strong cocktail would certainly help."

"Sure thing. You still drink whiskey and soda?"

"Yep. Some things never change, I suppose," Kerry said.

The two sat in the living room across from each other, and Kerry took a healthy swig of the cocktail his cousin had prepared for him. "Oh, man. That really hits the spot. Thanks, Jim." He had to admit it felt a bit weird sitting in the living room having a drink while his uncle's dead body was in the other room.

"This feels a bit . . . I don't know . . . surrealistic. Right?" Kerry said.

"Yeah, I guess it does. I'm still waiting for the reality of everything to hit me," Jim said, "I mean, I knew Dad was dying for some time, but now that it has finally happened . . . well, I suppose I'm still taking it all in."

Kerry asked, "You said you were going to tell me about the guy on the road. What's his story? And why did you say he wasn't there?"

Jim took a healthy gulp of his beer, then let out a deep breath and said, "Ok, here's the deal. I'm pretty sure you're going to tell me I'm full of crap afterward, but so be it. There was this guy who lived up the road a few miles, a rich guy named Sterling Caster. He was loaded but was also a bit . . . I guess you could say eccentric. He was this miserly sort who never spent a dime he didn't have to. One of his weirder quirks was he would walk up and down the highway picking up discarded bottles and anything that caught his interest."

"That is weird," Kerry agreed.

Jim continued, "Then he would take all the stuff he collected back home and separate it. When he had enough metal and glass bottles, he'd call a local rag man to come and pick them up. He'd get a few bucks for what he collected, money he certainly didn't need, but he'd tuck it all away in a drawer to eventually take to the bank."

"And he's still out there risking his life doing that for a couple of bucks?" Kerry asked.

"No . . . not really. Let me explain. Sterling started feeling severe pain in his hip, and after months of avoiding spending the money, he finally went to see a doctor who ran a series of tests, you know, x-rays and junk. They found out his hip was bad. This was back before they did hip replacements."

Kerry interrupted, "But they've been doing hip replacements for like fifty or sixty years. How could that be?"

"I'll get to that shortly. Anyway, his doctor told him that he wouldn't be able to walk along the highway doing what he loved to do because of his bad hip. Well, apparently, in his screwed-up mind, this felt like the end of the world to Sterling. So, one day, he went out and covered his car and himself with gasoline, climbed in, lit a match, and blew himself up."

"Are you trying to tell me . . ."

Jim said, "Yes. I'm telling you that what you saw and what I've seen myself on several occasions was the ghost of Sterling Caster walking along the highway. He's been sighted many times out there during the past fifty years. So, if you would have hit him, it wouldn't have mattered because he was just an image of a person, not a real, living being."

"That's ridiculous," Kerry insisted, "why didn't you ever tell me about this before? If that guy were a ghost, he would have been walking that road for more than fifty years, right? How come no one ever mentioned it to me before? I had been out here many times as a kid; why didn't I ever see him?"

"Maybe you did, but since you were just a kid, you probably paid him little attention."

Kerry insisted, "But I'm telling you, I saw him. He was there. He was alive as you or me."

"It might have seemed that way, but believe me, he wasn't," Jim said.

"I'll bet if I went out there right now, and he was still there, I could prove he was real. I'd just go grab him and bring him here to show you," Kerry said.

Jim said, "You probably don't want to do that."

"Why not? What's the big deal?"

"Well, as I said, he's been walking that highway as a ghost for more than fifty years. Local legend said he only shows up when someone else is going to die. The last time I saw him, a neighbor up the road passed away. I suppose he's become what they call a harbinger of death."

"So, you're saying I saw him because Uncle Fred was dying?"

"Yes."

"Sorry, Jim, I'm not buying this."

The sound of car tires crunching on the stone driveway alerted the two cousins to the arrival of the funeral director. Jim went to the door and let in two rail-thin, serious-looking men dressed in black suits, resembling the Crypt Keeper from the "Tales From The Crypt" television show. Kerry held back an inappropriate chuckle. The men wheeled in a cart with a long black zipper bag on top of it. Kerry immediately knew what that was for and wanted no part of any of this. He stood and quickly made his way to the front door with Jim following.

"Look, Jim. I, um . . . gotta go now. Call me and let me know the funeral arrangements. I'm staying in town at the Maple Tree Hotel."

"You can stay here if you'd like. I'd appreciate the company. We could catch up," Jim suggested.

"Um . . . Nah, I don't think that would work for me. Thanks for the offer, but sorry, no. I'll stop by tomorrow, and we'll talk some more."

Jim said, "Well, ok. But Kerry?"

"What, Jim."

"If you see Sterling again. Just pass him by. I can't think it would be a good idea for you to approach or connect with him. You know, the whole harbinger of death thing."

"You worry too much, Jim. Then again, you always were a worrywart. I'll be fine. Besides, you said he wasn't really there anyway, so no sweat, right?"

However, Jim knew his cousin and knew he wouldn't be able to pass up the temptation if he should happen to see the ghost again. Mainly because he never would believe what he had seen was anything other than a living man. That was how Kerry's brain worked. Everything was black or white, with no colors and no shades of gray. There was always an explanation for everything, including alleged ghost sightings.

Kerry drove carefully through the fog, watching for the crazy roadside garbage picker along the side of the road. He couldn't recall precisely where he had been on Iron Forge Road when he had seen the man. Part of his problem was the dense fog, and part of the reason was that Kerry was driving extra slowly looking for the man and had lost track of where he was. Just when he was about to give up, he saw a dark shape up on the side of the road, bent over, picking up something.

"There you are, you devil. Jim was wrong. I can see you as plain as day."

Kerry pulled his car over to the side of the road, got out, and stormed over to the strange man, shouting, "Hey buddy. What the hell do you think you're doing walking around out here in this fog? I nearly ran over you. Don't you see how dangerous this is?"

The man didn't reply. He just went about his business, picking up trash and loading it into a burlap sack he dragged along with him. Kerry became furious with the man, as there was little that he hated more than being ignored. He reached out to grab the man, saying, "Hey Pal, I'm talking to you."

But when he did, Kerry's hand passed right through the man's arm as if he consisted of nothing but smoke and shadow. At last, the man stood and looked directly at Kerry, standing stunned along the highway. It was then Kerry saw the horror of the man's scarred, burned, and disfigured face staring out through his hood with eyes that glowed like fire. The man's lips slowly curled upward into a wretched-looking grin as if to suggest he knew something Kerry did not, something the specter found humorous. That was when Kerry remembered his cousin referring to the ghoul as a harbinger of death. A moment later, he heard the blast of a car horn and the squealing of tires.

* * *

"What the hell was this guy doing standing along the highway in the fog, anyway?" The funeral home employee said to the funeral director as he bent down, examining Kerry's body. "God, I can't believe I hit him."

The funeral director said, "It wasn't your fault, Mark. He had no business being here."

Mark asked, "Is he . . . ?"

"Yes, he's gone. If it eases your conscience any, I can smell alcohol on him. He was probably loaded. It seems like nothing good ever happens out here on Iron Forge Road, not since that crazy old Sterling Caster burned himself up in his car."

"When was that?" Mark asked with a shaky voice, still shaken up from hitting the man.

"Nearly fifty years ago. I was on the call with the coroner. It was my first day on the job. Talk about trial by fire. Come to think about it, I believe it happened very close to here."

Mark stared down at the dead man with tears running down his cheeks, "God, why did he have to be standing here? I didn't see him, I swear. What could he have been doing out here?"

The funeral director stood and patted his assistant on the back, saying, "It doesn't matter, Mark. What's done is done. I suppose we'll never know." But he did know. He knew very well why Kerry had been out of his car because he, too, had seen the ghost of Sterling Caster several times in the past. The ghost always seemed to appear when someone was about to die. He supposed today was no exception.

Author's note: In January 2021, author/publisher and friend Mark Slade of Williamsburg, Virginia, proposed I write a story for a new anthology he was putting together with a bizarre premise. His idea was to take a story he wrote and give it to several authors, challenging them to write their own version of his story, blatantly plagiarizing his concept. The entire book would consist of plagiarized versions of his short story "Alt+Delete+Problem." Always up for a new challenge, I agreed. "Problem Deleted" was my contribution to the anthology.

PROBLEM DELETED

Two friends sat eating lunch in the tiny cafeteria at Strayer Entertainment. Strayer was a multimedia conglomerate known worldwide for producing animation for video games and developing advertising for virtually every form of media imaginable.

Derek Todd had something of a problem. For the past several months, Derek had been having trouble with one of the Strayer managers. The manager in question was the obnoxious mailroom supervisor named Bryan Keith, and had been a significant thorn in Derek's side. Because of an earlier incident, an accident on Derek's part, Bryan immediately disliked Derek. As a result, every day at lunchtime, the idiot would try to make Derek's life miserable by coming up with some new and agitating way of bullying him. Since Bryan was at the management level and Derek was but a pimple on the enormous backside of Strayer, there was little he could do about it.

The whole problem started one day when Derek accidentally spilled his drink on the lunchroom floor. As bad luck would have it, Bryan had been walking by, talking on his cell phone and not paying attention to where he was going. Bryan slipped on the spilled drink and fell flat on his bulbous butt.

He was not the sort of man who dealt well with embarrassment and always needed to have someone else to blame for his misfortunes. He had gotten it in his head that Derek had deliberately targeted him for God only knew what reason. So, being the complete idiot that he was, Bryan decided to make an example of Derek. Bryan was fond of saying, "I have a limited amount of power here at Strayer, but I do my best to abuse as much of it as possible."

Since that time, Brian would do anything he could think of to push Derek around, humiliating him at every opportunity. Sometimes, he would dump his complete lunch tray on Derek, pretending he had done so accidentally, yet laughing loudly so everyone around him knew it was deliberate. Other times, Brian would trip Derek, sending him crashing into other employees. He also enjoyed cutting in line in front of Derek, who had always meekly stood by and did nothing. Derek had considered taking his complaint up the ladder to Bryan's boss or the personnel department. Still, Derek had thought better of it after speaking with Sam and other Strayer employees. One of his coworkers said Bryan was "protected" and that he "must have pictures of his boss with a goat or something."

"Believe me, Derek," Sam said as he wolfed down his peanut butter and sardine sandwich. "I can help you with that douchebag." Sam glanced over his shoulder and saw Bryan staring a hole in Derek. "He's over there eyeballing you right now, Derek. What a dingleberry."

Derek swallowed a bite of his lunch and said with resignation, "I know. But what can I do about it? He's a manager, and he's protected. You know they watch out for their own around here."

"Maybe so, Derek, but I have ways of taking care of problems like Bryan, manager or not."

"Come on, Sam, you can't expect me to believe you can . . . what . . . wave a magic wand, and all my troubles will go away. Life ain't that simple, my friend, and we both know it."

"I'm telling you, I can do this. Look, dude. Remember how I got that promotion into the advertising department two weeks ago?"

"Yeah, of course. But what's that got to do with anything?"

"I got Jake Johnson's spot, right?"

Derek said, "Yeah, I remember. Didn't Jake Johnson quit and skip town or something goofy like that?"

Sam hesitated for a moment, then said, "Well . . . No, not exactly."

"What does that mean?" Derek asked.

Sam smiled, gave a strange little laugh, and said, "I'll show you what happened after work today."

"What do you mean you'll show me? What the heck did you do? Kill the guy or something? Are you going to show me a shallow grave in the woods or something?" Derek had started out joking, but now he didn't like the strange, distant, almost dreamlike expression on Sam's face.

Sam avoided the question and said, "Or something. We'll talk about it later. Hey, look over there."

Sam noticed Derek's former girlfriend, Amy, sitting alone at her favorite table. She appeared to be lost in thought, using her fork to move around the remains of whatever it was she had brought for lunch. He could see by the amount of food remaining that she wasn't eating. For whatever reason, she didn't seem to be very hungry.

Butting in where he had no business to do so, Sam said, "Look at her, Derek. You can see she's still really bummed out about you two breaking up. She's hardly touched her food."

Derek disagreed. "No, believe me, she's not even a little upset. Didn't you know she's been dating Wilbur Getty for the past couple of weeks? Believe it or not, he's even a bigger loser than I am. Hell, he may be even more of a loser than you are. And that is saying something." Derek couldn't help but laugh at his own barb.

Wilbur came in and sat down next to Amy at her table, and miraculously, her expression changed to one of happiness. She reached over Wilbur's lunch tray and gently rested her hand on his. Derek hated to see that, even though he had no right to feel jealous. They were no longer a couple. They weren't much of a couple even when they were together. They had never even gotten to the point of intimacy. Derek had been taking things slowly, being what his mother would call a gentleman.

He had been taking things too slowly, or maybe he would be the one sitting with Amy, and her hand would be resting on his. How was he supposed to know? The dating world had gotten strange. Whatever the case, he and Amy were a thing of the past, and she was now free to date whomever she wanted to. Still, Derek hated seeing her so happy with someone else.

He said in a mocking, condescending tone, "That stupid slob just cleans the floors in this building. He's a glorified janitor, for God's sake. I may not be an up-and-coming superstar, but at least I write copy for the stupid ads and ridiculous video games we make around here."

"You might not want to say that too loud. You know why." Sam pointed to a small black light fixture dangling from the ceiling. Then he whispered, "You know they watch and listen to everything we say around here. These people make Big Brother look like an amateur. And here's a fact you apparently were unaware of: Wilbur's job isn't cleaning the floors."

Derek looked up at the dangling fixture and said, "Seriously? Do you think the Strayer goblins are listening in on what we say? You gotta be kidding me, Sam. Look, if they were listening in, I wouldn't have cared less, but I'm certain they have neither the brains nor the intelligence to do so. I think it's safe to say that's nothing but a broken old light fixture dangling up there. I'm thinking maybe you should lay off all those energy drinks you've been pounding down. You're starting to get a bit paranoid. And what do you mean Wilbur doesn't clean floors? Amy told me he does, and that's his only gig around here."

"Sorry, Derek. She was only downplaying his role here at the company so that you wouldn't feel like such a loser. It's like this, Derek, my man. If Wilbur is a janitor, then maybe you can explain to me why I've seen him going into the game, developing offices and clocking in regularly."

Derek's mouth fell open in shocked surprise, and he asked. "He does? You actually saw that?"

"You bet I have."

"Well, maybe he's cleaning the floors in the gaming offices. Did you ever think about that? Yeah, I'll bet that's it," Derek said with hope in his voice.

"Sorry to burst your bubble, Bro, but that ain't the situation. The dude is a big-time developer and major coder."

Derek's heart sank as he and Sam watched Wilbur and Amy laughing together like a couple of conspiratorial lovers. For all Derek knew, they probably were lovers. Just because he and Amy never slept together didn't mean Wilbur hadn't gotten her to bed. If Wilbur's gig at Strayer was as crucial as Sam said, he might have literally charmed the pants off her.

Suddenly, a pad of butter flew past Derek's head and splattered against the wall behind him. Derek sprang out of his chair, trying to avoid getting splashed by the soft projectile, realizing the pad came from Bryan Keith's table. The jerk leaned back in his chair, giving Derek a toothy grin and flipping him the bird.

"What a dick," Derek said. "Ok, Sam, I'm in. What say I'll be at your apartment at six. You can show me what you have to solve my problem. That douche is going down."

"No, that's not gonna work for me," Sam said, shaking his head while gulping the remains of his second energy drink. "I better come to your apartment. I can be there around six. Chelsea's home tonight, and I certainly don't want her to see this."

Derek was still watching Bryan out of the corner of his eye, watching to see if the jerk was going to throw anything else. Then Bryan saw Derek staring at him and flipped him the bird again.

"Wow, that was original. Ok, fine!" Derek said through gritted teeth. "Let's go. I've had about enough of that dickweed for today anyway!"

* * *

Derek's apartment was what one might consider minimalist, not by design, however, but by financial necessity. There was nothing on the walls except for a picture of his grandma in an oversized frame. There was no furniture worth mentioning, save for a love seat Derek had scooped from a dumpster around the corner. There was also a worn, wobbly table in the dining area with two mismatched, equally wobbly chairs, where he sat with his laptop. His bedroom held only an old mattress, which served as his bed, and his childhood bedroom dresser he had gotten from his mother.

As the front door opened, Derek heard Sam complain, "That woman is driving me crazy. One of these days, she's going to make me do something I'll regret!" He handed Derek a USB plug, saying, "I told her I was just coming upstairs to see you, and she starts screaming at me like a banshee, complaining that I don't spend enough time with her!"

"What's this?" Derek said, ignoring Sam's rant and holding up the USB device.

"This is what I was telling you about at lunch," Sam said as he pulled up a chair and sat down. Then Sam noticed something on a nearby shelf and asked with a heavy sigh. "Let me get this straight. Even though this piece-of-crap chair is in such bad shape that it might collapse under me, break my spine and cripple me for life, you had money to waste on a Captain America doll?"

Derek looked at his latest prize up on the shelf and said, "It's not a doll, you goof. It's an action figure."

"Uh, ok. Po-tay-toe / po-tah-toe," Sam said, rolling his eyes.

"Whatever. Let's get on with this, ok?"

Sam looked around the room and said, "Uh yeah. I can see you're probably expecting a visit from the President any time now. Ok, down to business. You know how you've been having all that hassle from Bryan Keith?"

"Uh yeah. It's pretty hard for me not to notice. Nice of you to overstate the obvious."

"Well, this here little dongle is going to make all your problems go away."

"Seriously? How's this little gem going to solve my problem? Are we going to shove it down his throat and choke him to death?"

"That's harsh, dude, even for you. Look, just plug it in, will you? I promise it will work. There's a questionnaire you have to fill in. I'll help you with it."

Against his better judgment, Derek inserted the USB drive into his laptop. His screen went black, and as his eyes bugged out of his head, Derek shouted, "Did you just give me a virus? If you gave me digital herpes, Dude, I'll . . . I'll . . . I don't know what I'll do."

"Relax, you dope, I didn't give you any virus. Just hang on for a second," Sam said.

In a few seconds, the computer screen came back up, displaying a green background and a note in some sort of font that resembled an old English saying: PROBLEM DELETED.

"Ok . . ." Derek said cautiously. Then he asked, "So, the program is called 'Problem Deleted.' What now? I think maybe they could've invested a bit more time and made this interface look a little more interesting. It's a little on the boring side, don't you think."

Sam ignored his comment and said, "Just scroll down for a bit, and you'll see a highlighted link that says 'Tell Me Your Problem.' When you see that link, click on it."

Derek scrolled down, and when he found the link, he moved the cursor over it and then double-clicked it. The screen cleared, and a moment later, a questionnaire appeared.

"Fill that out," Sam said.

Derek asked, "How the Hell am I supposed to fill this form out? I don't know half of the crap they're asking me. I mean, his mother's name? Does Bryan even have a mother? I always figured something weird alien landed in his backyard to take a dump, and he was the result. Come on, Sam! What are you trying to feed me here? This is a bunch of nonsense."

Sam said with frustration, "Look, just go to his Facebook or Twitter feed. You'll find what you need there. People tell each other everything on social media."

"What do you expect me to do? Copy and paste his information? His profile ain't gonna have stuff like his mother's name. That's the kind of crap people use for passwords. And even a dope like Bryan probably isn't that stupid."

Derek rubbed the area between his eyes. He had a sharp pain in the middle of his forehead. He always got one there whenever he felt stressed. And whenever Derek found himself dealing with one of Sam's hair-brained ideas, he was guaranteed to find himself with a whopper of a headache.

"Don't be stupid. Go to either one of the social media sites or a search engine already," Sam insisted. "You won't be disappointed."

"I'll search for him on Google." Derek typed Bryan's name and was blown away by what he found. "Holy crap, he's all over the place. Just look at all the pictures of that stupid jerk."

"Let's try his Facebook account. It's usually the most reliable," Sam said.

Derek asked, "So how does this work? How does a program on a thumb drive solve my problems?"

"I don't know exactly. I think it links up with the internet and connects to a bunch of websites on the dark web."

"You mean like what . . . hit man for hire sites or some crap like that? I don't want to get involved with any hitman."

"No. I don't think so. Relax. It's more like dark, mysterious sites, like those featuring witchcraft or demonic junk. I don't really know."

"Uh . . . shouldn't we care about stuff like that, Sam? I mean, hit men are bad, but I don't want to go and sell my soul to the devil or anything like that."

"Geeze, Louise, Derek. Will you lighten up, for Christ's sake? I told you I've used this before, and it's ok."

Derek became curious, "So, tell me, Sam. How many times exactly have you used this program before?" Derek leaned back in his chair, staring at Sam. He suspected where this was all leading and saw a side of his friend he had never seen before. It was a much darker, much more sinister side.

"Honestly, I've used it several times," Sam said as he reached over and turned the laptop so it faced in his direction. And as you can see, I am still alive and healthy, and my soul is intact."

Derek wasn't exactly sure about Sam's last comment.

"Then, typing furiously, Sam said, "Here, I'll do it for you. So might as well, like I have to do everything for you."

"You don't do everything for me," Derek argued.

"I got you this apartment, didn't I?" Sam said.

"Well, yeah, I suppose you did. But in my defense, I wasn't able to help. Remember? I was sick, and my lease was up in two weeks. . . ."

"Blah blah blah. I even tried to talk to Amy for you."

"Maybe so. But a lot of good that did. I still managed to screw things up."

"It's a skill that, sadly, only you process. Someone might say you could screw up a one-car funeral. But, you know, it's never too late to fix things, my friend. I'm telling you, she still is crazy about you. I have no idea why. If you ask me, she'd have to be wacko to want the likes of you. I can't believe you weren't tapping that. I'd be all over that, first chance I got."

"Hey, man. That's just rude. Besides, you're happily married."

"Married, yes. Happily, not so much. Chelsea's always accusing me of cheating on her, and I never have. Maybe I should sometimes. Maybe with Amy."

"Now you're just trying to piss me off. Amy wouldn't give you the time of day. Besides, she's apparently come to her senses since she's now thanks to the wonderful Wilbur Getty. By the way, if he doesn't just clean floors, what exactly does Wilbur do at Strayer? Does anyone actually know?"

"I'm not really sure," Sam said as he turned the laptop around to face Derek once again. "As I said, I heard someone say he's a game developer, but I can't swear to it."

"He seems like a nice guy. He doesn't act like one of those developers. You know, they act like a bunch of arrogant, condescending jerkoffs."

"That's true. But to be honest, I'd probably act that way if I was a big-time video game developer. I mean, those guys are rock stars," Sam said.

"Wadda you talking about? You act that way now, and you're as big a loser as I am," Derek chuckled.

"Speaking of losers. You really should try to get back together with Amy. I'm telling you, Derek, she still has strong feelings for you. I can tell."

"No. Just forget about it."

"Hey, if you got back with Amy and started banging her, you could tell me about it, and I could, like, have vicarious sex."

"You are one sick and twisted human being, Sam."

"That's what you love about me and why we're friends. Birds of a twisted feather . . ."

"Forget it, Sam. Amy and me . . . we're history. I just don't feel like dealing with it."

Sam said, "Never mind, just press enter."

"Woah! Hang on a second! They want me to fork over three hundred and fifty bucks?" Derek shouted. "I ain't got that kind of cash. Hell, I couldn't even pay the WIFI bill or cable last month, and now they expect me to hand over all that money for what, this obvious scam?"

"It ain't a scam. Trust me. Besides, we both know you have money; you're squirreling it away," Sam jabbed.

"Hey, don't give me grief, Dude. That money is for emergencies," Derek complained.

"Wait a minute. You just said you didn't pay your cable bill? So, tell me, how the Hell are you still getting internet?" Sam looked at the lower right corner of the computer screen and saw the internet access icon belonging to his user name. Sam was furious. "Damn it, Derek! You cheap bastard. You're humping on my Wi-Fi. Pay for your own damned internet and stop leaching off mine."

"All right already," Derek said, feigning insult, "you don't have to go all psycho on me. Geeze!"

"Whatever! For now, look at the screen, and whatever you do, don't close the website! Ok, here's what you need to do right now. Just put that money into the 'Problem Deleted' tip jar, and we can get that mega-douche Bryan Keith out of your life forever. You know that's gotta be well worth $350. Use your PayPal account."

Then Sam suddenly got very serious and said, "Derek, you know I didn't have to show you this. If you weren't my bro, I never would have shared it with you. But you are in dire straits, my man, and unless you do this thing, that shaved ape is going to be back in the cafeteria looking for you tomorrow and every day after that. Now, do you wanna do this or not."

Derek began thinking about all the trouble Bryan could cause for the next several months. It did not make him feel warm and fuzzy.

With resignation, he sighed the pressed the Enter key. The computer screen displayed a bright red warning with an explanation that anyone using the program is forbidden from informing the media of the existence of the application. It further stated that the "donation" is not a payment for any illegal activities. It noted that neither party had committed any crimes. It said Derek's donation, minus minimal operating expenses, would be forwarded to a nonprofit organization dedicated to helping locate missing or runaway children.

"It's up to you now, Derek. Time to either defecate or vacate, as they say."

Derek reluctantly pressed the Enter key, filled in his payment amount, and pushed the Enter key one final time.

"That takes care of that, my man," Sam said with pleasure. "Bryan Keith is out of the picture."

"Suddenly, Derek felt a strange sensation in the center of his skull. I was like the distant sound of a thousand buzzing insects. It started almost silently, eventually growing somewhat in volume. Then he heard the faint cry of someone far away. It seemed like the person was suffering from incredible pain as his shouts turned to agonized screams. For a moment, time seemed to slow to a crawl, and Derek imagined a billion cells simultaneously exploding into the nothingness of microparticles as the scream eventually faded away to a whisper.

"You ok, Dude?" Sam asked, "You look a bit pale, even for you."

It took Derek a moment, then he said, "Um . . . yes . . . yeah, I'm . . . I'm fine. Just a bit weirded out, is all. Did you experience anything strange when you did this?"

Sam said, "Uh . . . no, not really. But you know me, Dude, I'm pretty cold. You are a much more sensitive sort of person."

"Yeah, I suppose you're right."

"Don't sweat it, Derek. That'll pass, I'm sure. Look at it this way: your troubles are over now. At least one of them anyway."

"Um, yeah, if you say so."

Sam replied, "I most definitely say so. Now, what say you get online and pay for your damn internet and stop being a mooching douchebag."

* * *

Sam's cell phone was ringing incessantly. His ringtone, "The Twilight Zone Theme," played repeatedly. Each time the ringing would start, Sam would let it drone on for half a dozen times or so before he'd finally disconnect it. Then he'd look over at Derek and shake his head in frustration. The two always rode to work together. Unfortunately for Sam, he got stuck springing for the gas fill-up that morning. He supposed it was his own fault. After Sam had shamed Derek into paying his internet bill, Derek had apparently become strapped for cash and didn't have any money left for gas, or so he claimed.

Sam still didn't completely buy the sob story Derek was handing him. It sounded like a steaming pile of road apples to Sam. But he nonetheless stepped up and bought the gas.

They eventually arrived at work on time and walked grudgingly down the hallowed halls of Strayer Entertainment, inching their way into the elevator that would ultimately take them to their offices, which they thought of as slave pits.

"Aren't you ever going to answer your stupid phone? It's really annoying," Derek asked in a semi-whisper, not wanting to start an argument in a crowded elevator. He knew Sam would have no problem causing a scene. He lived for that sort of drama, while Derek hated it.

"Nope," Sam replied, looking at his phone again before shoving the phone into his coat pocket. Then he looked around the elevator to make sure everyone could hear him perform and said, "I have no intention of answering the damned thing all day."

"Why not?" Derek asked, still trying in vain to keep the conversation private.

"Uh . . . because I don't want to . . . duh!" Sam grumbled.

Finally, Derek had enough of Sam's antics, and crowd or not. He said, "Hey. Don't jump down my throat dickweed. It ain't my fault you're on the rag. So, how about you at least silence the stupid thing! The damn thing is giving me a headache."

"I have no intention of doing that either," Sam said, "so you might as well get used to it. And by the way, that's Mr. Dickweed to you."

"Sam, I swear, if your phone goes off one more time . . . so who's been calling you anyway?"

"It's Chelsea, okay?" Sam said much quieter; now, he was the one who wanted the conversation to return to private mode; then, he looked away from Derek, somewhat embarrassed.

"Your wife. That Chelsea?"

"Uh yeah," Sam replied sarcastically. "My wife. The only Chelsea we both know."

"You mean the same Chelsea who hates my guts?"

"Yes, Derek. The same. Then again, she pretty much hates everyone's guts, so don't let it make you feel so special."

As the elevator doors thankfully slid open, the two friends squeezed past several other riders to exit. When they did, they saw Amy jogging up to the elevator. She stopped outside, deciding it was too crowded.

"I guess I'll catch the next one," She said. As she stepped aside, she dropped everything she was carrying, including an apple, which rolled along the floor and ended up at Derek's feet. Derek picked the apple up and handed it to Amy, feeling the uncomfortable, awkward moment when their eyes met. The tension in the air was thick enough to cut through.

"Uh," Amy said as she accepted the apple and adjusted her glasses. "Thanks . . . Um, Derick. Sorry, I . . . I guess I didn't have time to eat breakfast this morning. I was running a bit late."

"Oh," Derek nodded, feeling tongue-tied. "I see." He did his best to hide his discomfort by acting as coolly as possible but failing miserably.

"Sam," Amy said in a curt greeting.

"Amy," Sam replied equally curtly.

Sam's phone began to ring again. He stared ahead, pretending not to hear it ringing.

"Sam . . . Your phone is ringing," Amy said, stating the obvious.

"He knows," Derek said, still feeling uncomfortable with the encounter.

"Oh. Ok." Amy looked somewhat confused, then decided it might be better not to ask.

"So, when are you going to tell me, Sam? What happened between you and Chelsea?" Derek asked when the phone eventually stopped ringing.

Amy seemed interested in the conversation while simultaneously trying to look like she didn't care.

Sam hesitated, then said, "It's stupid. Chelsea's paranoid. She thinks I'm cheating on her. She accused me of it when I got back from your apartment. I told her she was nuts. We had a big blowout! I got a bit crazy, stormed out, and stayed at a hotel last night.

Amy looked at Sam oddly. Sam looked away quickly, but not before Derek noticed the exchange. He decided he imagined things, and it was all part of the discomfort he was feeling with Amy so close.

"Why didn't you just stay with me?" Derek asked, even though he was secretly relieved that Sam didn't choose to stay over.

"You gotta be kidding! I mean, thanks for the offer, but I had no intention of having to deal with your heinous foot stench. Thanks, but no thanks," Sam joked.

Typically, Amy would have chuckled at this and nodded her head in agreement. But something was off with Amy; Derek could tell. He gave her his most curious stare, and she looked down at her feet as if embarrassed.

"You didn't tell Chelsea that you were coming up to my place before you left?"

"No," Sam said defensively. "It was none of her business anyway. I told her she could do what she wanted, and I was going to do the same."

"Seriously, Sam? That was so retarded," Amy said. Sam turned and stared daggers at her. "Ok. Sorry. None of my business either," Amy said as she bit her lower lip and once again stared down at her shoes.

"Sam, you know Amy's right," Derek said.

"What? You're going to take the advice of some former girlfriend who can't even manage to hang onto a loser boyfriend like you?"

"Hey!" Amy shouted, now becoming angry. It was strange how Amy and Sam couldn't seem to maintain eye contact.

Amy turned her anger on Derek, "I don't need advice from either of you, especially not from Mr. 'I don't have time for a relationship.'"

Derek stood speechless with his mouth agape.

Sam shouted, "You two are both losers! You two are the ones who should be married. Not me and Chelsea. You're both perfect for each other! You're both weird!"

With that, Sam walked out, leaving Amy and Derek standing and silent in their awkwardness.

* * *

Sam and Derek sat silently at lunch, not speaking to each other. Instead, they watched their coworkers eat and chat with each other. Sam noticed that Bryan Keith wasn't in the lunchroom.

"Hey," Sam said as he tapped Derek on the knee.

"What?" Derek was shocked to hear Sam speaking to him. He wasn't mad at Sam anymore but was surprised because Sam always tended to stay angry longer than he did.

"Did you happen to notice somebody is missing," Sam said. Derek shrugged and went back to concentrating on his lunch. Sam sighed with frustration and tried again. "Derek?"

"What, Sam?" Derek said.

"Damnit, Derek, I'm trying to tell you something!" Sam said.

"Tell me what?" Derek asked.

"I said, did you notice anyone missing from the cafeteria today?"

"No," Derek said, shaking his head. "What are you talking about?"

"Take a look around and think about it for a second. Who is usually in here busting your balls whenever you try to eat your lunch? Any name comes to mind?"

The realization hit Derek like a ton of bricks. He had been so busy stewing over the strange exchange between himself, Sam, and Amy that morning that he had forgotten about his problem. His eyes grew large with the realization. "Woah! Bryan Dickwad Keith?"

Sam said with a sly smile. "Yeah, Bryan Dickwad Keith."

Derek stopped smiling. "You're not serious, Sam. He probably just called off sick or something."

"When was the last time Keith called off sick or even missed a day of work? That obnoxious load is like always on the perfect attendance list."

Derek started smiling again. "Yeah, you're right. The douche is a boy scout when it comes to showing up for work. So you mean to say that website actually worked . . ."

"Shh! Don't. . . ." Sam looked around to make sure no one was listening. "Don't say it. Don't even think about talking about it unless we're alone. Remember?"

"Oh," Derek said, recalling the warning on his computer screen, then nodded in agreement, "Yeah, I forgot. Sorry, you're right, Sam."

"Of course, I'm right, numb nuts. When are you going to get it through your thick head that I'm always right?"

Then Derek recalled the strange sensation he had experienced after pressing the enter key for the final time. He recalled the buzzing, the screaming, followed by nothingness. A cold chill ran down Derek's spine, and he shivered.

Sam saw this and asked, "You ok, pal?"

"Yeah, yeah, I'm fine. Just had the weird feeling again."

Then Derek looked across the lunchroom and saw Amy sitting with Wilbur Getty. However, that didn't keep her from glancing over at Derek and Sam occasionally. Did he imagine things, or did she seem to be looking more at Sam than at him?

As Derek asked himself that question, the company's executive director, Mr. Charles Gallagher, and two men in gray overcoats approached the table where Wilbur and Amy were sitting and began speaking with Wilbur. After a few seconds, Wilbur got up and started to leave with them. Amy watched them go, then sat alone, looking very concerned. Sam sprang from his seat and approached Gallagher as they headed toward the door.

"Mr. Gallagher," Sam called out, "Hey! Mr. Gallagher!"

Gallagher turned and looked hard at Sam. Not only was Gallagher Sam and Derek's boss, but he didn't like Sam. As far as Derek was concerned, Gallagher had no idea who he was or that he was even a subordinate.

"What is it, Johnson?' Gallagher growled. He never called Sam by his first name.

"Uh . . . sir . . ." Sam chuckled.

"Well?" Gallagher asked with growing frustration. "Spit out, Johnson! I don't have all day!"

"That position . . ." Sam said, but Gallagher cut him off mid-sentence.

"There are two things you should already know by now." Gallagher rolled his eyes, let out a sigh, then continued, "One: as long as I am executive director, you will never, I repeat, you will never, ever be a manager in this company. You are an extremely pushy, obnoxious, self-centered young man and are far more annoying than any sane person could tolerate. I wouldn't put you in charge of cleaning out our urinals. And two: that position has been eliminated."

"But it's still up on the corporate website. I saw it this morning," Sam tried to explain, but once again, Gallagher cut him off.

"We don't need that position as long as I'm running things! Besides, I already have my assistants." He jerked a thumb towards the two men in overcoats. "They are my eyes and ears in this world. Do you understand what I'm saying, Johnson?"

Sam nodded, then looked at the two men and said, "Yes, I suppose I do."

"Now," Gallagher said, "do us both a favor and get lost. I have more important things to take care of."

* * *

Derek was busy playing video games when he heard a loud, rapid knocking on his apartment door.

"I wonder who that can be," he threw his game controls on the floor. "I'm coming, I'm coming already. Hold your damn horses."

Derek opened the door to find Sam standing there, looking stressed and more than a little concerned. "Oh man, Derek. I did something horrible."

As Derek shut the door, he said, "Take it easy, man. Deep breaths. Now calm down and tell me what happened. You didn't kill Chelsea or anything like that, did you?" Although Derek was saying this in jest, part of him was still concerned. He knew his friend; he knew about the Problem Deleted program and understood Sam wasn't always rowing with both oars in the water.

Sam looked directly into his friend's eyes and confessed, "Or something," His voice had a frightened tremor to it.

Derek was becoming genuinely concerned now. He asked his friend directly, "What are you saying, Sam? Did you leave her?"

Sam shook his head. He appeared to be losing control. "No, no, I didn't leave her, Derek."

Derek suddenly had an epiphany, and the idea chilled him to his very soul, "Oh . . . no . . . please, Sam . . . please tell me you . . . you . . . didn't?"

"I did," Sam whispered as he hung his head in shame, tears running down his cheeks. "I . . . did. And . . . and I feel incredibly horrible about it."

"Oh, my God," Derek said as he sat down hard on the couch. "You . . . you should feel horrible . . . this . . . this has got to stop, Sam. You can't just keep making people vanish. It's . . . it's like murder, Sam."

Sam sat down next to Derek, crying like a baby as he ran his hands through his hair. "I know," he scarcely was able to squeeze out.

"So, you're telling me you used that damn program on your wife, and now you're saying Chelsea . . . no longer . . . exists?"

"Yeah, Derek, Chelsea . . . no longer exists."

"This Problem Deleted thing has become a real problem for you, Sam."

"Yeah," Sam said through his tears. "I . . . know, I know, Derek."

"Why in the name of God would you do such a thing?"

Sam shrugged his shoulders and wiped at his streaming eyes. "She wouldn't stop bugging me. She was accusing me constantly."

"Um, ok. That makes perfect sense, NOT! What the Hell is wrong with you, Sam? I know you're not on crack, and I'm fairly certain you're not completely retarded. At least, I don't think you are. Maybe you're just a psychopath . . . I don't know."

"We . . . we were fighting again. Same crap over and over. She wouldn't let up."

"So, what 'crap' was the fight about this time?"

"It was about Amy," Sam said.

"Amy? Why would you two be fighting about Amy?"

"Well . . . I sort of . . . um . . . screwed Amy, and Chelsea found out about it."

"You what?" Derek was in shock, certain he had heard wrong. "How the Hell do you 'sort of' screw Amy. You either did or you didn't. There's no 'sort of about it, Dude."

"Ok. You're right. Yeah, I banged her . . . that night after I left your place and walked out on Chelsea."

Derek remembered the strange look that had passed between Sam and Amy outside the elevator at work and how he caught her looking too long at Sam in the lunchroom. His stomach turned in disgust.

"And you thought I would be good with this, why?" He shouted at Sam.

"No, I knew you wouldn't be, and that's what makes me feel so bad. I mean, I know you two aren't dating anymore, but you both still have, you know, feelings for each other."

Derek retorted, "So let me get this straight. You delete your wife out of existence. For some reason, you don't have a problem with that, even though that's the equivalent of murder. But you feel terrible about plowing, Amy. You are one sick puppy, Sammy, old boy. Do you know that?"

"Look, Derek. I didn't mean for that to happen. It just did. It was sort of an accident."

"Accident? What accident? Did she slip, fall, and a strategic part of her anatomy land on a certain part of yours? Was that the sort of accident you had, Sam?"

"No, it was like this . . . I went over to Amy's apartment to talk. You know, just to get her to take on my marital issues."

"So . . . you just . . . decided it would be a good idea to screw her . . . Amy . . . in her bed?" Derek was getting angrier by the second. The thought of Sam taking advantage of Amy, his Amy, made him furious. So maybe he didn't have the right to think of her as his Amy any longer, but he still did.

"No. Not in her bed," Sam said.

"Oh, that makes me feel so much better." Because Derek never had sex with Amy when they dated, Sam's casual way about what he did only served to make him crazier.

"You know . . . we talked a while. A good while. We watched some TV and ate some nachos."

"She made nachos for you? Well, why didn't you say so sooner? I suppose if she made you nachos, then you were entitled to bang the doors off of her," Derek said sarcastically.

"I know you're mad, Dude. I get it. As I said, I didn't mean for it to happen. She bent over in front of me to clean up the nacho plates, and I . . . well . . . I couldn't help myself. I'm sorry, Derek, but I had to tell you. It happened so fast. One minute, she was bent over in front of me, and the next thing I knew, her skirt was up, and she was begging me not to stop. So, I didn't. After it was over, I just went home. I was ashamed and still am."

Derek didn't say a word.

Derek wasn't listening.

Derek was beyond listening.

Sam left the apartment.

* * *

Derek stared at his laptop screen. He was in the Problem Deleted program. Sam had forgotten to take the thumb drive with him the night he left. Derek had all of Sam's information entered into the questionnaire. He had paid his $350 and had his finger on the enter key, yet something prevented him from pushing it. Sam had both helped Derek during their lives and caused him far too much pain. The fact was, Sam was an immature, selfish douchebag and always had been.

Before she had married Sam, Chelsea had gone out with Derek several times. Then, one time, they met up with Sam and his then-girlfriend at a restaurant. Sam hogged the entire conversation all evening long like he always did. The next day, Chelsea stopped returning Derek's calls. The next thing he knew, she and Sam were married.

Despite all this, Derek couldn't bring himself to push the button.

"Why can't I do this? Sam deserves it!" He wondered, struggling with the decision, thinking about Sam and his Amy coupling like two rutting beasts.

Then Derek's phone suddenly rang. He looked at the screen and saw it was Sam. He didn't want to answer it, but he did nonetheless.

"What?" Derek barked into the phone.

"Hey, Wilbur called me," Sam said. In his anger, it took him a moment to recall Wilbur.

"So what?"

"He wants to talk to us."

"I don't want to talk to him," Derek said. "I don't want to talk to you either, for that matter."

"Hey, Buddy . . . look, I know you're upset . . . I told you how sorry I am . . . I can't apologize enough . . ."

"Yes, of course, you can. You can apologize from now until the end of time . . . 'buddy' . . . but your words mean nothing to me."

"No . . . look, you don't understand. We've both used that app, Derek. We're both guilty. Never mind. Listen, just come to the park today, okay?"

"No. I'm not going anywhere with you, Sam."

"Derek, they're going to kill Wilbur," Sam shouted.

Derek was shocked. "What are you talking about? Who's going to kill Wilbur?"

"Come with me to the park, and you'll see."

Derek said, "I don't want to go. I don't want to be part of any of this anymore."

"I'll meet you there in fifteen minutes," Sam said as he disconnected the call.

Derek became so furious he threw his cell phone against the wall. It ricocheted backward and hit the shelf holding the Captain America action figure. Then as if in slow motion, Derek not only saw it falling but saw the trajectory in which it was traveling, right for his keyboard.

He screamed, "Noooooooooo!" as he tried to reach his laptop in time. But like trying to run in a nightmare, Derek's feet felt like he was stuck knee-deep in thick muck. When his hand was just inches away, Derek saw Captain America's red, white and blue shield hit, then press down the Enter key. The screen went black for a moment. When it returned, a box appeared in the center of the screen, informing Derek that his request to remove Sam from existence was approved.

Deep in his mind, Derek heard the distant buzzing of a thousand insects as he had last time, but now they were growing even louder in volume by the second. Then the screaming began, not only more audible than before but far too familiar. He had an image flash into his head, and visualizing it almost made his mind snap. It was Sam, his best friend, standing in a room alone, screaming at the top of his lungs as his body disintegrated into a billion dust particles.

"Oh my God, no. What have I done?" Derek cried as he fell to his knees, buried his face in his hands, and wept uncontrollably.

* * *

Derek walked robotically around the park, looking for Wilbur. He wasn't even sure why he had come. He had just killed his best friend. His former girlfriend had cheated on her current boyfriend. Now he was wandering in a park looking for that current boyfriend, who he really didn't know or care about that well. Derek headed toward a cluster of bushes behind a basketball court when he saw them move.

"Derek," a voice called out to him. "Psst! Derek," the voice was strained. "Over here! In the bushes."

Wilbur popped his head out from the middle bush, waived to Derek, then quickly ducked back down.

"What's going on, Wilbur? Why are you hiding in the bushes?"

"Shhhh! Don't. Keep as quiet as you can."

"Okay. So, what's going on?"

"Where's Sam?"

"He said he'd meet me here, but . . . uh . . . I suppose he didn't make it after all. You know how unreliable Sam can be," Derek said, hoping Wilbur had bought the lie. The truth was Derek was a mess over what he had done to his friend. Derek didn't know if he would ever be the same again. All he could think of was Sam's dying screams.

"You weren't followed, were you?" Wilbur asked.

"What? No. I mean, I don't know . . . I don't think so. Who would be following me?"

"Gallagher and his cronies," Wilbur whispered. "You don't understand; they're going to kill me."

"Kill you? Why would they want to kill you, Wilbur?"

"Because of the program . . . the one called Problem Deleted," Wilbur confessed.

"You know about that program?"

"Know about it? Hell, I'm the one who created the software and figured out how to access the dark web as well."

Derek was shocked. "You? You did all that?"

"Yeah. But to be honest, now I wish I hadn't. After I realized the program actually did what it was designed to do, I had to find a way to stop it. I decided to encode the software with safe chips so that I could start controlling who could use it and how they might use it."

"How did Sam get a hold of the program?"

"Sam? Oh crap! That's where that got to," Wilbur said.

"What do you mean?"

"I had a rough prototype of the program. It's locked and can't be edited or anything, but apparently still works fairly well. I guess Sam must have stolen it from my office."

"That was sort of sloppy on your part, Wilbur."

"Yeah, I suppose it was. If you get your hands on it, destroy it, ok. There is only one other copy, and that is the one that can still be modified."

"I gotta ask you, Wilbur, why the Hell would you create a program like that in the first place?" Derek asked.

"It was supposed only to be a simulation to be used as part of an upcoming video game, but somehow it became so much more. Even I have no idea why it's capable of making individuals disappear. Then, like an idiot, I showed the program to Gallagher. Maybe I was trying to score some brownie points or something, you know, sucking up to the big man. Anyway, he used the program to eliminate his competition and get to where he is now in the company. Then the board of directors of the company found out about it . . . and now, because I'm trying to render it harmless, Gallagher is after me."

"Why don't you get on the program and make Gallagher and his toadies disappear? Or, for that matter, why doesn't he just get on and use it on you?"

"That's a good question. Part of the reason is we can't use it on each other. They took care of that when they made me rewrite the code and tag people who can't be deleted. That's what the safe chip is all about. Gallagher is one of them who can't be deleted . . . VPs, board members, the president of the company, and me. Oh, and Amy, too. I added her as well, and not just because we're dating. You see, the other reason they can't use it on me is they don't have the program. They think I do. But the truth is, I never got to finish the safe code.

"So, I turned the program over to Amy. She's been involved with the program since the start and knows almost as much about the program as I do. However, Gallagher doesn't know about Amy's involvement. But it will only be a matter of time until he either finds out or figures it out on his own. That's why I need to ask you a very important favor. I need you to make sure she and the program are far away from here, someplace where Gallagher can't find her. She's going to render the program useless."

"There he is!" A voice shouted. Derek looked out and saw Gallagher and two men running through the park. The two men ran past Gallagher, and Derek panicked, ducked, and covered his face with his hands. He heard three sets of footsteps running past him. Derek spread his fingers slightly to see that the two men were chasing Wilbur, firing their guns at him in broad daylight. He couldn't believe it was happening.

The first two bullets whizzed by Wilbur's head as he ran toward a shallow man-made pond. The two men fired again. This time, both shots caught Wilbur in the back. He fell face-first into the pond, blood streaming out of his wounds, turning the clear water at first pink, then crimson.

Derek turned back to see Gallagher walking purposefully in his direction. Derek sprinted through several bushes and out of the park, continuing for several blocks before realizing no one was following him.

* * *

Derek stood in front of Amy's apartment, pounding on the front door. He heard the sound of her unlocking several of her locks before the door opened slightly.

"Derek?" Amy gasped and unfastened the chain from the door. She opened it quickly and pulled Derek inside.

Amy was in her nightgown and socks, her hair pulled back in a pony-tail. Derek had never seen her like this. He stared at her for a moment and thought about what he had missed while they were dating. He had been so naïve when it came to relationships. He had thought he was being a gentleman. But now, after hearing what Sam had told him, all Derek could think about was Amy and Sam doing the deed right there on the coffee table in front of him. How could he have been so stupid?

"What are you doing here, Derek? It's two in the morning?" Amy asked angrily.

"Amy. Listen to me. We have to leave," Derek said in a panicked voice. "They are going kill us, and we have to get out of town!"

"Derek, calm down," She insisted. "Have you been drinking?"

He grabbed Amy roughly by the arm and pulled her toward the front door. "Listen, Amy. We need to get to your car! I'll explain along the way."

Amy pulled her arm back, "Stop this, Derek! I'm not going any-where with you. Are you nuts? You know I need my sleep. I have to be at work in the morning . . . and so do you."

"No! Listen to me. Gallagher is going to kill you! He's already killed Wilbur! I saw his henchmen do it earlier today. I've been hiding since this afternoon, waiting for dark so I could come and get you."

"What? Wilbur . . . dead?" Amy said in shocked disbelief as she sat down hard on the sofa. She began to shake as she sobbed with her head in her hands. Derek sat beside her and wrapped his arm around her.

"Yeah, and believe me, I'm so sorry, Amy. I've never been so scared in my life. There were these two men in black coats with Gallagher. They came running after us, waving guns. I went one way, and Wilbur went another. I heard two gunshots. When I looked back, they were fishing Wilbur's body out of the pond."

"Why? Why would Gallagher . . . why would anyone want to hurt Wilbur?" Amy asked, choosing off sobs.

"Something about a safe chip for Program Deleted application."

Amy said, "Derek, that's what I've been working on for Wilbur, and I'm almost finished. Are you saying the company doesn't want the safe chip on the application? I mean, this is all fictional, anyway. Not worth killing anyone over. Wilbur told me this program was a precursor to the company's new video game. He said he needed to make sure some people couldn't be deleted from the game. You know, so that they could essentially play the game without worrying about being killed. I mean, let's get serious here, Derek; no one can use a software program to make real, live people disappear."

"It works," Derek said.

"What do you mean it works?"

"The program, 'Problem Deleted,' can really delete people. That's why Gallagher is after it and why he killed Wilbur. And that's also why Wilbur added himself and you to the safe code."

"Are you telling me . . ."

"Yes. That's exactly what I'm telling you. This program can actually delete people. I have no idea how it works or why it works, but I'm telling you this program can take people out of existence."

"That's . . . that's ridiculous, Derek. Besides, how would you know anyway?"

"Well, I've used it, Amy. Sam showed me how. He stole an early version of the program from Wilbur. We . . . we used it on Bryan Keith."

"You're not serious, Derek, are you? You can't believe that."

"Yes, of course I do. Have you seen Bryan around lately? Have you noticed him harassing me in the lunchroom like he always did?"

"No. I suppose I haven't seen him in quite a while. This is all starting to sound really weird, Derek."

Derek nodded his head and agreed. "Yeah, really weird. Weirder than you might imagine. Before he was killed, Wilbur asked me to get you out of town to somewhere safe so you could destroy the program once and for all. I really need you to come with me, Amy."

They sat in silence for a bit. Derek gave Amy time to take in all he had told her. Finally, Amy leaned in and kissed Derek. He didn't react at first. He was too shocked. Then he realized he was staring at the coffee table and imagining Amy and Sam having sex right in front of him.

"What?" Amy asked. "What's wrong, Derek? I thought you liked me."

"I do, Amy. There's nothing wrong with you," Derek replied, getting up from the couch. He couldn't consider restarting a relationship with Amy, not after what he knew, "There's something wrong with me."

She rolled her eyes and said, "Oh wow. That's the oldest trick in the book, Derek. 'It's not you; it's me.' Come on, Derek, I'm not a baby. Can't you just be honest with me? Just this once?"

"Look, Amy. I no longer feel the same way about you as I did before. Things have changed. I've changed, and how I look at you has changed. I just can't think of you romantically anymore. I still care for you but as a friend."

"Wow, another stereotypical putdown. 'Can't we just be friends?' Seriously? Come on, Derek, can't you be a little more creative than that?" Suddenly, Amy was furious. Her face twisted into a hideous beet-red expression, the likes of which Derek had never seen before. "Fine, that's the way you want to play things, then forget it."

"Amy, please listen to me . . ." Derek tried to calm her.

"Get out!" She screamed.

"What?" Derek was shocked by her hostile reaction. "You don't understand; I have to get you out of here, to safety . . . Wilbur asked me . . ."

"Get out of my apartment now!" Amy screamed again, tears streaming down her face. "I don't ever want to see you again."

Without a word, Derek turned and left. He walked down the apartment hallway and got into the elevator. He walked out of the apartment lobby and out onto the sidewalk. He stood at the curb for a moment, watching an old man and woman getting into a cab.

A moment later, Derek heard the sound of a thousand insects buzzing inside his head. He felt incredible searing pain as if every cell in his body was on fire and torn apart. He heard screaming and realized the cries were his own.

* * *

Amy took her finger off the Enter key. A window popped onto the screen, telling her that Derek Todd had been deleted. She felt no remorse for what she had just done. She felt an incredible sense of satisfaction. She closed the lid on her laptop. She had already decided the program was too important to destroy. She was already thinking of how she would finish encoding the safe chip on the Problem Deleted application in the morning but would be removing several key people from the safe list.

DARK IS WHERE THE MONSTERS DWELL

"Deep into that darkness peering, long I stood there,
wondering, fearing, doubting, dreaming dreams no mortal
ever dared to dream before."
—EDGAR ALLAN POE

"When the darkness comes, keep an eye on the light—whatever
that is for you—no matter how far away it seems."
—JAN BERRY

"Walk while ye have the light, lest darkness come upon you."
—JOHN RUSKIN

"For the love of God, Ed, you're 57 years old. Don't you think it's far past time you learn to sleep without a nightlight?"

On a Saturday morning, the couple sat at the breakfast table having a somewhat heated discussion about an old, worn-out topic that had been a bone of contention for many years. But now, for Sylvia Blankenship, this problem had come to a head. She was going to take a stand to make sure it was resolved once and for all. She knew her husband was not going to make things easy for her.

"For the thousandth time, Sylvia, it's not a nightlight; it's a security and safety light. You know how clumsy I can be. If I have to walk to the bathroom in the middle of the night with our cats and dogs skulking about, that light is the only thing saving me from a broken neck. You wouldn't want me to fall and break my neck. Would you?"

"No, of course not. Don't talk such nonsense. You're my husband, and you know I love you. You also know I would never want anything bad to happen to you. Don't think for one minute that I don't see what you're trying to pull here. I've been married to you long enough to know all your tricks. Right now, you're deflecting."

"Deflecting? Me?" Ed said with feigned innocence.

"Yes, you. Because you don't want to deal with your ridiculous fear of the dark, you deflect and try to turn it on me. Well, nice try, Bubba, but I'm not going to let that happen. We both know it's way past time we deal with this, Mr. Edward Charles Blankenship. And by 'we,' I mean 'you' have to deal with this. You're not five years old anymore, Ed. You're just a few years away from retirement, and yet you still have to sleep with a nightlight on."

"I've told you a million times, Sylvia, I am not afraid of the dark. I'm just not very comfortable with at least a little bit of light available. It simply makes life easier and safer."

But Sylvia knew Ed was lying both to her and himself. She had been married to him for 37 years and had heard every one of his lame excuses. "I have poor night vision. It's not safe walking in the dark. I might trip." Blah, blah, blah. She had tolerated it all during the early part of their marriage. She supposed she had chosen to "go along to get along" during the rest of their time together. But lately, she had found as she had gotten older, she was having more difficulty getting a good night's sleep, and having Ed's "safety light" blasting its blinding beams like a New England lighthouse did little to help her situation.

"Ed, the bathroom is ten feet away in a straight line from your side of the bed. There are no obstructions in your way. If you need to use it, all you have to do is get out of bed and walk straight to it in the middle of the night. For God's sake, Hellen Keller could find her way; it's so easy."

"But the animals . . ."

"No buts. The dogs are in bed with us most of the time, and the cats will run out of your way. All you have to do is shuffle."

"What if I have to go downstairs for some reason?" Ed said, trying lamely to strengthen his argument.

Sylvia countered, "We have motion-activated night lights in the hallway and all over the place downstairs. They can stay where they are.

It's just that stupid beacon of glory you keep lit in the bedroom that has to go. You know I've been having a terrible time sleeping lately."

She had tried several over-the-counter sleep aids but to no avail. Whatever the cause of her sleep issues, Sylvia had concluded that Ed's infernal obsession with having some form of light available 24/7 was, at least, a contributing factor. So, she decided before she went to the doctor for a more substantial prescription sleep aid, this was one variable she had to remove from the equation. Besides, she felt it was ridiculous that she needed to address such a topic with a man his age.

Although Ed may have been deflecting, if not blatantly lying to his wife about his fear, he most certainly was not lying to himself. He knew inside he honestly was terrified of the dark, and more importantly, Ed knew why he was frightened and had known the reason all his life. Early on in his younger days, he thought he might not be able to live with this knowledge; however, once he discovered what a valuable weapon light was, he found a way to deal with it . . . with them.

Back when Ed was a child of five, his grandmother had told him, "Edward, be careful, my boy. Watch out for the darkness because the dark is where the monsters dwell."

He had never been a fan of the dark before that, but hearing those terrifying words from an adult, his grandmother no less, only made things worse. Had that proclamation been the end of it, young Eddie believed he might have been able to outgrow his fear. However, once he saw them, the things that live in the darkness, all bets were off.

At a family weekend gathering, he, his younger brother, and his parents stayed at his aunt Shirley's home in western Pennsylvania. Eddie was about eight years old at the time. At first, he was excited about visiting his cousins, then after they arrived, Eddie learned that all the kids would be sleeping together in the family room on the floor on blankets.

His cousins were older than him, and Eddie knew they would not use a night light. That meant he would have to sleep in the dark, which frightened him to no end. However, there was also a television in the room. That would provide enough light to help him fall asleep. He didn't understand precisely how this monsters-in-the-dark thing was supposed to work, but he believed as long as he was sleeping, they couldn't find him. He figured it had something to do with the idea that if he saw them, it would give them the ability to see him as well.

Eddie had fallen into a sound sleep that night while his cousins watched a late-night scary movie. He had hoped they, too, would fall asleep with the TV on, which would be as good as a night light, maybe better. But as bad luck would have it, they turned off the TV when they decided to go to sleep, plunging the room into total darkness. Sometime during the night, young Eddie woke up to find himself in a world of blackness. That was when they came.

He pulled his blanket up over his head, allowing only the tiniest space for him to look out, although Eddie had his eyes tightly closed and didn't plan on looking at anything. That was when he heard the noise: a slimy, slithering sound like that of a dozen giant snakes crawling on the floor next to him. He opened his eyes a little, just enough to see through the crack in his covers. His mind screamed at him not to look, reminding him over and over about how curiosity killed the cat. But nothing could stop him. He had to know, and he had to see for himself.

What he saw was a horror so incredible that it burned itself deep into his psyche. The trauma was so severe that even after a lifetime of rationalizing and trying desperately to convince himself the experience had all been a product of his young, vivid imagination, adult Ed was still terrified of the dark. Looking out through the tiny fragments of space in his covers, little Eddie had seen one of them.

It crawled slowly in the blackness, its presence visible by the subtle yellow-green glow of its reptilian skin. It slithered low to the ground, resembling an almost flat disc, with just the trace of a mound to show its elliptical shape. It was as long as a good-sized dog from end to end, and Eddie was having difficulty making out any face on the thing. Along the creature's base were what appeared to be thousands of leg-like appendages, which reminded Eddie of those he had seen on centipedes. They were apparently what moved the creature along the floor. The slithering noise must have come from the monster's underbelly as it scrapped along the bottom.

Two foot-long antennas extended out from what Eddie believed was the front of the thing. On the ends of each of those antennae was an eyeball. The long appendages constantly moved in slow, circular motions as the eyes scanned the area, searching for something. Eddie believed he knew what that something was, or more accurately, who that someone was. He was confident the creature couldn't see him, yet somehow, it knew Eddie was watching from somewhere nearby. It was as if the monster had some sense that humans didn't possess. He had recently learned about the five senses in school. But this thing in the dark seemed to have some awareness that went beyond any of those senses.

As the monster passed by Eddie's line of sight, the creature raised itself on long, front muscular legs that seemed to extend out from below the creature's underbelly, appearing as if from nowhere. The legs looked almost human except for the oversized, ape-like feet, with sharp claws on the end of extra-long toes. Underneath the monster, a huge mouth opened to reveal a cavernous maw filled with rows and rows of overlapping shark-like teeth. A stench flowed from the opening, like his family's garbage can stinking on a sweleringly hot summer's day.

The creature's two eyes moved in Eddie's direction, then stopped as they met his for just a second. Yet, Eddie knew that a single second of eye contact was long enough. Eddie heard a high-pitched, whining sound coming from the beast. It started as a faint keening sound but quickly became an ear-splitting cry. Soon, Eddie heard other cries as more of the heinous monsters slithered over toward him. Eddie screamed in terror, waking up all the cousins who slept near him. One of them turned on a nearby light, and they saw Eddie cowering under the blankets, sobbing and trembling uncontrollably.

The noise had been loud enough to bring his mother and his Aunt Shirley down to the family room. Adult Ed couldn't remember anything else about the visit other than it had been cut short because of his trouble. He did, however, recall the realization he came to that night. Even at such a young age, Eddie understood if the creatures couldn't see him seeing them, they couldn't find him or hurt him. They also couldn't come around as long as some form of light was present.

He believed that making eye contact with the monster that night somehow marked him. They had seen him; they knew him and now knew who he was. He also believed they could and would find him again if he gave them the opportunity. Fortunately, his family had decided to head home early and leave that day because he didn't think he could have survived another night in the dark. If he didn't have a source of light to cut through the darkness, sooner or later, the monsters would find him again, and those rows of razor-sharp teeth would be coming for him.

Now, after more than five decades of sleeping while having some form of light available, Ed realized he might have to face his greatest fears again. Would the creatures still be there in the dark waiting? Had they ever really been there at all? Was it possible that this life-long fear had been the result of a bad dream he had experienced? His cousins had been watching a horror movie. Maybe he heard it in his sleep, which was the catalyst for a nightmare. He did have quite the imagination as a young boy. In fact, he still did.

Ed recalled other times over the years when he would lie in bed, sure he could hear slithering noises out in the blackness of the darkened upstairs hall. Had he been dreaming then as well? Indeed, if creatures were lurking in the hall, wouldn't the dogs and cats have known it? People always said animals were sensitive to things humans couldn't see. And wouldn't the movements trigger the motion-sensitive night lights out in the hallway? He had no idea and no answers. These were not new questions for Ed as he had asked them of himself many times before. Yet never during the past almost fifty years had he ever tempted fate or tried to sleep in total darkness again.

So why did he feel so guilty about having the light? What did it hurt to have a bit of light? As he told Silvia on many occasions, the light kept him from tripping or stubbing his toe in the dark. What was wrong with that? But she was having a lot of trouble sleeping. His light didn't help her situation any, and she did seem determined to make him give up his precious illumination. As Ed walked up the stairs to get ready for bed, he suspected he would have to face his fears momentarily. When Sylvia made up her mind, it became law carved in granite.

As he suspected, when he entered the bedroom, Ed looked over and saw the nightlight, which he had plugged into the wall outlet on his side of the bed, was gone. He looked over at his wife, who was already in bed with her head propped up on her pillow, reading a book with the light on her nightstand on, pretending she wasn't watching him. Ed noticed his nightstand light was missing as well. Sylvia was determined he would not be using any light whatsoever.

Sylvia looked up from her reading and said, "I told you this night-light nonsense had to stop, Ed, and right now is as good a time as any."

"But Sylvia . . ."

"No buts, Ed. I've made up my mind. From now on, there will be no more nightlights in our bedroom. You might as well get that through your head once and for all. I need my sleep, and dammit, I'm going to get it."

"What about my reading light on my nightstand? You still have yours."

"Sorry, Ed. You gave me no choice, at least for now. You're going to have to go cold turkey tonight. I couldn't risk you going for the reading light. Honey, I have faith in you. You can do this, Ed. I know you can.

Ed said nothing. What could he say? He had no idea what to say. Sylvia had laid down the law, and he felt a bit embarrassed by the entire situation. She had been so patient with him over their long years together. He supposed he owed this to her. But what if it hadn't been his imagination? What if the horrid creatures were real? What then?

Sylvia had returned to her reading, which meant he would have light for at least a bit longer. He crawled into bed, turned his back to Sylvia, closed his eyes, and, luckily, was soon fast asleep. Sometime after midnight, he awoke and opened his eyes to total darkness. At first, a feeling of panic began to take over, and Ed decided he should get up, shuffle to the bathroom, close the door and turn on the lights until this panic attack was over. But just as he was about to get out of bed, he heard the slippery sound, like something slimy oozing across the floor.

Even after so many years, Ed recognized that sound immediately. It was them, the creatures of the darkness. They were here in his bedroom, slithering around on the floor beneath his bed. He smelled a vile stench emanating from the floor, a reek he likewise still recalled from decades earlier. He could hear the steady breathing of his two dogs, sound asleep between him and Sylvia. He also heard the soft, gentle, motor-like purring of two of their three cats somewhere on their bed.

"What the Hell is wrong with these animals? How can they be asleep? Can't they hear these monsters? Can't they smell them?" Ed wondered in astonishment and horror as he lay on his back with his eyes still pinched tightly shut. That was when he felt a tug on his covers down by his feet.

He thought, *Maybe it was Mittens, their third cat pulling at his covers, or perhaps it was Ginger, their golden retriever tossing in her sleep and pulling at his blankets.* His typical night was often an ongoing tug-of-war with his animals for the comfort of covers. But as he listened, he realized none of the cats nor dogs was near his feet. The sound he heard from the bottom of the bed was much too liquid for any typical animal. That was when he understood what it was that he was climbing up into his bed and onto his feet.

Ed lay perfectly still, too terrified to even move a muscle; his eyes clamped tightly closed as something pulled itself up into the bed. He was stunned to realize the thing seemed to have almost no weight as it reached his feet. The foul stench grew more potent, and Ed could feel thousands of gently moving things scurrying up along his legs, feather-light. His heart hammered in his chest as the crawling sensation crept over his stomach and toward his chest.

He wanted to shout, to scream out for Sylvia to turn on a light. But so many thoughts ran through his mind at once. If he called and Sylvia answered, would the creatures go after her as well? If he remained silent and kept his eyes shut, would the monster pass him by and move on? Was any of this actually happening, or was he sleeping and having an incredibly real yet simultaneously surreal nightmare?

Ed felt the tickle of a dozen tiny feet on his chin. His heart was pounding so hard, and he was sure it would explode in his chest. That was when he felt two strong hands pressing down on his chest. He recalled the two human-like arms he had seen as a child, jutting out from the monster's underbelly. Those two muscular arms were now pressing down on his chest. The sudden downward pressure was robbing him of his precious air, suffocating him. Still, Ed kept his eyes shut, even as he broke out in a cold, sopping sweat, and excruciating pain suddenly shot down his left arm. He opened his eyes and looked up into a horrifying, stinking, elliptical maw filled with hundreds of pointed teeth and a long reptilian tongue coming ever closer to his face.

* * *

Sylvia awoke in the morning to dulled sunlight creeping in through the cracks alongside her room-darkening shades. She could make out the silhouette of her husband, Ed, lying on his back next to her.

"You did it, Ed. I knew you could. You made it through the night without that stupid light. You should be proud of yourself, Ed . . . Ed? Ed?"

She reached out and touched his face, only to find it ice cold. Then she saw the expression on her husband's face. His eyes were bulging outward in terror from his dusky, gray, and obviously dead face. That was when the screaming began.

HOT TUB

"I can't believe these people and what they've let happen to their house!" Jay Frederick complained to his wife, Helen. The couple was standing on their beautiful, covered patio adorned with plenty of comfortable furniture. They were looking over the privacy fence at the house next door. Their backyard was their paradise, overflowing with beautiful flowers and blossoming trees, a coy pond filled with fish, a fire pit with circular stone seating, a two-person swing, and last but far from least, an outdoor kitchen. Birds by the dozens flew to the many feeders they kept well-stocked with seed and made good use of the more than twenty birdhouses Jay had built and placed around their yard.

However, the same could not be said of their next-door neighbors' property. To say their neighbors' home was a disaster and an eyesore was an understatement. The six-foot privacy fence surrounding the property was of excellent quality and was still in surprisingly good condition after a decade, at least on Jay and Helen's side. However, what existed on the other side of that fence was anything but acceptable.

Tall mature pine trees surrounded the property and were planted along the inside perimeter of the fence, providing an additional layer of privacy and blocking the views of curious neighbors. Unfortunately, that also offered these less-than-desirable neighbors the opportunity to allow their property to become overrun with weeds. In addition, it meant their cleaning up the stinking land mines left by their aged, half-blind, completely deaf dog became optional. This was not appreciated when the summer temperatures scored into the nineties.

Helen replied, "I know, Jay, but there's nothing else we can do about it." She said, "We've spoken with the township supervisors every chance we could over the last decade, and they all said the same thing."

"Yeah, I remember. Oh, how I remember. They said those people were not violating any township ordinances. Sure, their house might need some maintenance, but the township doesn't get involved unless we can prove it's a danger to the public. We had the same message from the homeowner's association."

Along the side of Jay's neighbor's home was a pile of old, broken, discarded yard furniture, haphazardly stacked and practically covered over with years' worth of weeds. The metal items within the mess were coated with rust, while any wooden pieces were rotten and crumbling. Those few formerly white vinyl chair remnants were green with mold and creeping vines. The house's roof was in disrepair, and the gutters were being held crudely in place with rusted wire. They looked as though they might collapse at any second.

Helen said, "The township supervisors told me the last time I called them that unless their concrete sidewalk was broken or damaged to the point where someone walking by might trip and fall, they could do nothing. And even if it were broken, they would only address that single issue with them and none of the others. One of the township supervisors had the nerve to suggest that the only reason we're complaining is that we earn good incomes. He said because of our joint incomes, we can keep our property in pristine condition, and as a result, we set the bar too high for people with average or lower incomes."

Jay argued, "He has no damn idea what he's talking about. Pulling weeds is free. Cleaning up dog crap is free. Hell, washing the mold off your vinyl siding only involves a little bleach in water. There is so much they could do if they weren't so damn lazy. Besides, if they couldn't afford to live here and maintain their property, why did they buy the house in the first place? God, I thought the people who owned the house before them were bad: Ken and . . ." Jay snapped his fingers, trying to remember his former neighbor's wife's name.

"Sandy. It was Ken and Sandy."

"That's right. But I always called them Ken and Barbie because they reminded me of those stupid dolls," Jay said.

Helen said, "Remember how they were always trying to outdo us? But I didn't mind most of the time. It meant they were at least keeping their property in good condition. The only times I questioned their decisions were when they were blowing their money on stupid things that they thought would make them look as if they were doing better than us."

"Yeah, like that ridiculous hot tub," Jay said. "A lot of good it did them. When the market crashed, and Ken lost his job, they went bankrupt, got divorced, and ended up selling the place to those Beverly hillbillies next door, and we've had to live with them for the past decade or more. We had to sit back and watch their property go downhill every year and pray it didn't take our home's property value with it."

"I worry about that all the time. It really concerns me," Helen confessed.

Jay said, "There's one thing these two idiots next door did that I can't understand. Ken told me before he moved out that when the two mutants next door bid on the property, they demanded the hot tub remain as part of the deal. Remember me telling you that?"

"Yes, sweetie. I remember."

"Yet that eyesore has been sitting there in the backyard, disconnected for more than a decade. No one ever used it, not even once."

"It's terrible," Helen agreed, "I remember even back when Ken and Sandy lived there, they hadn't used the thing for two or three years. It's probably got the same water stagnating in it for over ten years. Surely, that must qualify as some sort of health hazard."

Jay looked at his wife in amazement, "Babe, that's an incredible idea. You're a genius. I can guarantee you the lid to that tub hasn't been removed in more than thirteen years. That means the water is likely contaminated by God only knows what sorts of disgusting microorganisms. I remember once when Barbie and Ken still lived there . . ."

"It's Sandy and Ken," Helen corrected.

"What?"

"Our old neighbors . . . they were Sandy and Ken, not Barbie and Ken."

"Whatever. Anyway, I remember when Ken called me over to look at something in the hot tub. A squirrel must have climbed up the wooden side of the hot tub, crawled under the cover, and drowned. The thing was all swollen and bloated. Ken had to fish it out with a pool net. Do you remember that?"

"Yes, Honey, I remember you telling me about it after it happened. You were pretty grossed out, as I recall."

"You're right about that. It was a disgusting sight to see. Now think about it for a moment; if one squirrel had managed to get under that cover, then it stands to reason that other animals may have found their way inside. That cover is nothing more than one inch of foam padding covered in cheap vinyl. Hell, a chipmunk or squirrel or even a field mouse could easily chew through it."

"Yes. You're right, Jay."

"And think about this. That water has been lying stagnant under that cover for like thirteen hot summers and frigid winters. I'll bet there are colonies of disease-carrying mosquitoes in that water right now. God only knows what new biological infections are growing in that primordial stew."

Helen asked, "So, what do you think? What's our plan?"

"I think if I wait until it's dark and the neighbors are busy watching evening game shows, I could sneak over with a glass jar, lift the cover and scoop out some of that hot tub goo. Then we could have it tested to see exactly what new infections are growing in that oversized Petri dish."

"Yeah, that's a great idea. Then, we could take a copy of the report to the township supervisors and the homeowners association. Once they see what a cesspool that hot tub is, they'll have to see things our way. But do you think you should go anywhere near that thing without a hazmat suit?"

"Good point. I probably should at least get some heavy-duty long rubber gloves if I'm going to be getting a sample of that water. Maybe a surgical face mask like we started wearing during the COVID pandemic and still occasionally do."

"Yes, that's a good idea."

"And I'm going to need you with me."

"Wha . . . wha . . . what? M . . . me with you? I'm sorry, sweetheart, but there's no way I'm putting my body anywhere near that stinking hot tub."

"I didn't expect you would, nor do I expect you to do so. You will be my lookout. I need someone to keep an eye out for anyone while I get my samples. You can stay right inside the gate and watch along the side of the house. You'll be a good twenty feet or more from ground zero."

Helen looked perturbed and said, "Bad choice of words, Jay, and not appreciated."

Jay chuckled, "Yeah, um, sorry, Babe."

"So, when are you planning on doing this, Jay?"

"As soon as possible, my dear. I'm going to head to the hardware store right now for something to gather my specimen and to get some good PPE."

"PPE? What's that?" Helen asked.

"Personal Protective Equipment. You know, like scaled-down hazmat stuff. Not industrial grade but good enough for our needs."

"So maybe tonight?"

Jay agreed, "Not maybe, but definitely. Tonight will be as good as any night and probably better than most." He looked down at his smartphone and pressed a few icons on the screen, saying, "Looks like tonight will be warm, and there will also be a full moon. That means plenty of moonlight."

"Honey, are you sure about this?"

"Of course, I'm sure, Helen. We need the authorities to see what a mess that place is, and if getting a water sample will make them sit up and listen, then all the better. If all it does is force them to get rid of that mosquito breeding ground, they call a hot tub, then fine. But if we're lucky, they might notice what a dump the place has become, and maybe it will cause them to take some action against them. You know, make them clean up a bit."

"We can only hope so."

A short while later, Jay returned from the local home center. After dinner, he checked to make sure he had everything he needed to get his water sample. He had a glass jar with a screw-on lid, the kind used for jarring preserves. He had heavy-duty black rubber gloves which extended up past his elbows. He also bought a pair of leather electrician's gloves, although he had no idea why he had bought them or how they might help him. He looked out the window and saw the sun was setting and said, "I'm ready to do this thing, Babe are you?"

"I suppose I'll never be ready for something like this, Jay. But I'm willing to do my part for the good of the team."

"Then let's go over and gather the evidence we need to rid ourselves of our troubles."

Before Helen could speak, Jay was on his way out the French patio doors and heading for the side gate. He whispered, "Come on, Baby. Time's a wastin'. We need to get over there, pronto."

Helen followed reluctantly, wearing a black jacket and a dark blue scarf covering her hair. She had on a pair of dark sunglasses as well. To the casual onlooker, she resembled some famous Hollywood actress trying desperately not to be recognized. At least some of that assumption would be true, save for the part of her being a famous Hollywood actress. Helen most definitely didn't want anyone to recognize her.

She stood just inside the neighbors' gate, watching the street as well as the neighbors' house for any activity. Jay was already next to the hot tub. He wore a dark hoodie that he had on under his well-worn North Face jacket, the hood tied securely owner his head.

I told him to throw that horrible jacket away two years ago. I guess I'm glad he held on to it, Helen thought.

Jay had on a transparent face shield under which he wore safety goggles and two layers of surgical masks. Thick black vinyl gloves protected his hands and halfway up his arms as well. He carefully lifted the front corner of the hot tub cover with his left hand as he prepared to dip the jar into the water to get his sample.

For a second, Jay had to stop to gather his resolve and fight the urge to vomit. He dropped the hot tub lid back into place and backed off a few feet. Even from her location more than twenty feet away, Helen could smell the stench that rose from beneath the cover. She supposed the lid must have formed some sort of airtight seal over the years, which must have kept the horrible pall from escaping previously.

It indeed was revolting, worse than anything Helen had ever experienced. The stench was a combination of stagnant water, some gross fishy stink, and something resembling the foul aroma of dead animals baking in the hot summer sun. She couldn't believe her husband was about to dip his hand into that filth. Rubber gloves or not, there was no reason for him to risk possible contamination.

She whispered, "Jay . . . Jay . . . let's forget it. You don't need to do this. We can just complain to the township about a bad order coming from the place, and they can find the mess. Let them bring in a hazmat team."

Holding back his need to retch and taking a few gulps of precious fresh air, Jay said quietly, "No . . . no sweetie . . . it won't work. They won't come . . . They're going to need proof before they even consider coming to investigate. I have to get that sample no matter what."

"But Jay, that God-awful stink. Who knows what diseases are festering in that cesspool."

"Please, Babe, just watch out for people. I'll make this quick."

Before she had the chance to argue further, Jay had lifted the cover once again and dipped the glass jar into the water below, pulling it out filled with a dark, murky-looking liquid. Helen watched her husband gently set the hot tub cover down and screw the lid back onto the jar. She didn't know what she had been expecting to happen; she supposed she feared the liquid in the tub might be like some horrible acid that would eat through Jay's glove and dissolve his hand or something.

Helen could see Jay's eyes smiling behind his face shield and safety glasses in the moonlight. He said, "See babe, it was easy peaz . . ."

But, before he could finish his sentence, the cover on the hot tub flew open, and Jay felt something slimy yet powerful wrap itself around his throat. He heard Helen gasp and saw something beyond his ability to imagine. She, too, was in trouble. A long, tentacle-like length of something as thick as a man's wrist and more than twenty feet long had somehow traveled the distance across the yard in two seconds and encircled Helen's throat, as it was doing to his own. The massive arm was dragging Helen across the yard by her neck, pulling her toward him.

Jay grabbed the tentacle surrounding his throat, trying desperately to break its grip. However, the thing was too strong, and he was encumbered by his rubber gloves, the thing's slimy exterior, and his ever-decreasing oxygen supply. Just before he lost consciousness, he was lifted upward and over the edge of the hot tub. The last thing he saw was Helen's feet as she went under the stagnant water, and then he felt the terrible cold as he followed.

The evening was calm and still now, with barely a sound save for a few night insects buzzing. Thick, black, slime-covered tentacles gently placed the cover of the hot tub back into place as the moon reflected off a broken glass jar on the patio beneath the hot tub.

DEAD THINGS

It was an irrational fear; he knew that. It would have seemed ridiculous to most people, a fact of which Kevin was sure. But for him, it was as natural, as acceptable as breathing. The simple truth was he hated dead things.

Most people might say, "So what? No one in their right mind likes dead things. Why would they? Besides, how many times in your life will you encounter something dead anyway?"

Kevin knew exactly how often people encountered no-longer-living creatures, and it was a lot more often than he suspected most people ever realized. For example, many people might drive down the highway, see a dead, bloated groundhog swollen in the hot summer sun and pay it little or no mind. Or they might see a cluster of turkey vultures feasting on a dead deer in a cornfield and ten seconds later forget they even saw it. Some might even run over rabbits or squirrels and not even take time to feel bad about it. If a bird glanced off the side of a vehicle, many people would worry more about any damage to their paint job than the fact that they just killed an animal. Kevin estimated that the average commuter might see five or more dead things every day.

That assessment only covered members of the animal world. It didn't consider human beings. We, of course, all die, and although we may not be left to rot by the side of the road, death does eventually claim each of us. When we least expect it, we each must deal with the occasional dead friend or relative. And Kevin understood that each year, as he aged, those numbers increased proportionately. Kevin had to develop clever excuses to explain his lack of attendance at their funerals whenever one of these untimely misfortunes occurred. The simple truth was that he hated being anywhere near dead things.

He once researched the internet and found something very close to what he felt. It was called Necrophobia. The web described it as an irrational fear of dead things. It also described Necrophobia as fear of different things that we associate with death, such as funeral parlors, graveyards, and such. This was where the definition got a bit fuzzy for him. He had no fear of tombstones, funeral services, caskets, or cemeteries. Neither did he fear his own death. He didn't believe in ghosts, nor did he believe the dead could harm him in any way.

In his opinion, Kevin's severe displeasure when near-dead things weren't what he considered a fear at all. He believed it was more like an uncontrollable disgust with the former living. Dead things made him nauseous and nervous and overwhelmingly revolted.

It had been that way with him since he was a little boy, and it seemed to grow stronger and more of a crippling problem the older he got. The first time it happened, he had been about five years old. He and several of his neighborhood friends were outside walking around one summer day when they came upon a dead rabbit in the street. The other kids were curious about the creature but not Kevin.

All he could see was a squashed, barely recognizable mound of fur and violently exploded guts. Shiny blue-black flies covered the rotting carcass. There were also dozens of tiny white worms he would later learn were called maggots. The stench of the creature was revolting, a stink that he would never forget for the rest of his life. One of his friends found a long stick and tried to pick up the rabbit's entrails while several other kids laughed. Kevin turned and fled around the corner, only stopping long enough to puke his young guts out. He knew he would surely get grief from the neighborhood kids, but he didn't care.

Since then, there have been many other encounters with dead things, and none of them ever ended well. Several years earlier, Kevin was called upon by his wife to remove a dead bird from a birdhouse in their backyard. The front part of the dead bird's body was sticking out through the entrance hole.

Kevin had not wanted to deal with it. He had made it clear to his wife many times how he felt about such matters, but eventually, she persuaded him to remove the poor creature. Reluctantly, he found a long, needle-nose pliers in his toolbox. It was an old, slightly rusted tool, which was good because he planned on throwing it away as soon as he did what he had to do.

He walked up to the birdhouse with a paper bag in one hand and his pliers in the other. He slowly reached up and gripped the dead bird's beak in the tool's jaws, then began to pull the bird's body from the house. For a moment, he feared he might pull the thing's head off. He didn't know what he would do if that happened, but fortunately, the extraction went flawlessly. That was until Kevin heard a flapping above him as another bird flew from a tree, divebombing him and barely missing his head. Because of his tension over removing the dead bird, he had been wired tighter than a high E guitar string, and that unexpected bird dive was enough to snap that string. Kevin had stood half bent over in the yard as a tremor raced from his head to his toes.

He dropped the bag, the pliers, and the dead bird as he waited for the uncontrollable shivering to stop. When it did, he staggered to his house, took a double shot of whiskey, and went to bed for the rest of the day and didn't come out from under the covers until the following day. That nervous reaction and several others over the years, which proved to be even more crippling, happened whenever he came into proximity of anything dead, whether it be animal or human.

After a time, Kevin found a way to get his Necrophobia, or whatever his problem was called, under control to a degree. He had accomplished this by not only avoiding being near anything dead but also by distracting himself. For example, if he were driving along a country road and saw a dead squirrel flattened on the highway, he would look away and try to do some math problems in his head. If that failed, he would fire up his car stereo and start singing along to any of his favorite songs. If he didn't know the words, he'd make them up—anything to keep him from fixating on the dead thing.

He could often be seen driving along the road with his radio or CD player on ear-piercing volume, singing along at a near scream in a desperate attempt to take his mind off whatever horror he had just witnessed. To the casual observer, it might have appeared that Kevin was a music fan and enjoyed his tunes. He might even have looked crazy to some people, but Kevin didn't care. He did whatever he had to do to get by.

He often wondered what would happen if he confronted his problem head-on and forced himself to be near something dead. He might get sick; in fact, he probably would. But maybe if he did it often enough, the sickness and trembling might slow down or even stop. But he never tried to see if such a drastic action might work. He suspected that one of these days, he might have to give in to his wife's insistence and see a counselor.

Most recently, his aged blind and deaf golden retriever had gotten even sicker, and Kevin knew the dog was going to have to be put down. He knew he could not handle being present at the event, let alone dealing with disposing of the body once the deed was done. Kevin had planned with his veterinarian, Dr. Harry Wilkins, to have old Duke cremated. And, of course, he had no desire to take possession of the ashes as they were essentially only one step away from being dead things themselves. Dr. Wilkins assured him that the $300 fee he paid would take care of both the cremation and the disposal of the cremains.

On the day of the euthanization, Kevin dropped the dog off at his vet, paid his fee, and drove away as quickly as he could. He loved that old dog, and after leaving the office, he had become overcome with sorrow and had to pull over to the side of the road, where he sobbed uncontrollably. He also hated that he couldn't bring himself to be with Duke during his last moments. He had always heard that being with your pet at that final time was extremely important, but doing so was something beyond his capability. Doing what he had done made Kevin feel weak and less of a man. He was disgusted with himself while at the same time understanding because of his affliction.

A few days after dropping Duke off with the veterinarian, Kevin was sitting on his front porch on what turned out to be a sweltering hot afternoon. He was drinking a cold beer and thinking about old Duke and the issues he had dealing with dead things. By now, old Duke would be ashes likely scattered to the winds. Kevin still felt terrible about not being with his old friend at his final moments, but it was what it was. As he sat with his eyes shut, hoping for an afternoon nap, Kevin heard approaching footsteps coming rapidly up his sidewalk.

He opened his eyes and saw his friend and neighbor, Dave Harper, hurrying toward him. The man looked both terrified and worried.

"Dave, what's up, brother? You look upset."

"I am Kevin. It's my dog, Bo. He's missing."

Kevin was genuinely concerned, having just lost his own dog. "Missing? How long, Dave?"

"A few hours. He got out of our back gate. The lawn guy must not have closed it properly, and Bo ran off. We think he might have headed into the woods behind our house."

"Jeez, I'm sorry to hear that, Dave. What can I do to help?"

"I was just heading out into the woods to look for him, but Sarah yelled at me and said I shouldn't go alone. She thinks I might trip and break an ankle or something. Can I trouble you to help me look, Kevin?"

"Of course, you can. It's no trouble at all. I know how important animals are to us. You know we had to have old Duke put down earlier this week?"

"No, I didn't. Gosh, I'm so sorry to hear that, Kevin."

"Thank you, Dave; it was a tough thing to do, as I'm sure you are aware. But right now, I think we should focus on finding Bo and bringing him back home."

"You're right. I truly appreciate your help."

Kevin got up from his chair, placed his empty beer bottle on the porch, and said, "We'd best be heading out there and start looking for your pup. The sooner we get started, the better."

The two men walked into the woods together, calling for Dave's missing dog, and were having no luck when they came to a Y intersection where the path split off in two separate directions.

They both stood silently for a few seconds when Kevin asked, "Do you have any idea which direction we should head?"

Dave looked from one path to the other and said, "I . . . I suppose . . . actually, I have no idea which path to take. I've never been this far into the woods before. I think maybe we should split up and each take a path. We can search separately, and if either of us finds him, we could call the other. You have your cellphone, right?"

"Yeah, and it looks like I have full service, at least for now."

"We'll probably be ok for a while. I doubt we'll have to go much further. Bo has never been in these woods before, and I doubt he would stray very far. I can't imagine it will be much longer until one of us finds him. I just hope he's ok. That's my real concern."

Kevin said, "Don't worry, Dave. Bo's a smart dog. I'm sure he'll be fine."

"I certainly hope so. We'd better get moving."

Kevin headed down his path, calling for Bo as he walked. Dave did the same, walking along the other path in the opposite direction. It didn't take long before Dave's fading voice vanished completely, and Kevin knew they would need to communicate by cell phone moving forward. He looked at his phone again to verify he still had service, and fortunately, he did.

Rounding a turn on the path, Kevin came upon a fenced-in area with a gravel road leading up to it. He assumed the road must have come in from the state highway, which he estimated was probably nearby. If he listened carefully, Kevin could hear the occasional car horn or revving engine in the distance, confirming for him that the highway wasn't very far away. He hoped Bo hadn't strayed down the gravel road and out onto the highway, or else he might be struck and killed by a speeding motorist. Just the thought of Bo's dead body lying along the road caused Kevin's legs to tremble slightly.

In front of him, the eight-foot-high fence had two large gates centered on the gravel roadway. They had a chain and padlock holding them shut to automobile traffic, but they hung open enough for a man or dog to squeeze through. A large red and white metal sign hung secured to one of the gates. It read, "Property of H. Wilkins. No Trespassing. Violators Will Be Prosecuted to The Full Extent of The Law."

Kevin said, "H. Wilkins? Harry Wilkins? My veterinarian? Dr. Harry Wilkins? I had no idea he owned land out here."

Suddenly, Kevin heard a sharp bark coming from inside the fenced-in area. *Bo?* Kevin thought, *That's Bo's bark, I'm sure of it.*

Ignoring the warning sign, Kevin squeezed between the gates and ran toward the sound of the dog's bark. He didn't travel far before he saw Bo, a black Lab, standing next to what appeared to be a ravine. The dog was visibly upset about something, and his frantic barking only served to accentuate his distress. He kept looking alternately between Kevin and the hollow, like he wanted Kevin to see something. It reminded Kevin of those ancient reruns of that show, Lassie, where the collie would bark to get people to follow her whenever little Timmy got himself into trouble and fell down a well or something stupid like that.

"What do you want me to see, Bo? What do you have there?"

The dog lowered his head and started to whine with one of the most mournful cries Keven had ever heard. As he took a few steps closer, Kevin was hit with a familiar and horrifying smell. It was an odor he knew too well, a stench he spent his life avoiding. It was the pall of purification. Something was most definitely dead in that hole just a few feet away. All the warning alarms in Kevin's mind began to go off simultaneously. Maybe Doc Wilkins had come out here to his property for some relaxation, then had a heart attack and died. Perhaps he fell into that ravine and was decomposing. But if that were the case, wouldn't his car or truck be nearby? There was no vehicle by the gate when Kevin came through.

Maybe, kindly, old Doc Wilkins wasn't so kind after all. Perhaps he was a serial killer and had bodies buried in that ditch. Kevin's imagination began to run rampant. Kevin moved closer against his better judgment, perhaps because he could see Bo was in distress. When Kevin reached the Bo, the dog rubbed his head against Kevin's leg and keened pitifully. Suddenly, dozens of crows and turkey vultures took flight in a cloud of black. Kevin looked down into the pit, and his stomach lurched with the ungodly sight before him.

The pit overflowed with dozens, if not hundreds, of animals, primarily dogs and cats, in various stages of decomposition. What looked like millions of flies covered the rotting carcasses and hovered all about them. Among the dead, a few of the less intimidated crows and vultures continued to tear meat from the bodies. Then Kevin saw something that made his blood, which was already running cold, turn to ice. On the top of the pile was his dog, Duke.

The pitiful creature's body had been ravaged. His eyes had been plucked from their sockets, and his skin and fur were torn off in places where the carrion eaters had most recently fed. As if all of this were not enough to fray Kevin's last nerve, he saw the ID tag he had personally inscribed for his beloved dog dangling from the neck of that mangled corpse. Kevin looked at Duke's face through tearful eyes and saw a bullet hole in the center of the dog's skull as he was on the verge of passing out.

Then, the realization hit him. Doc Wilkins had been swindling all the good people of Kevin's community. He charged them $300 to euthanize their animals and then cremate them to give them a peaceful farewell. In some cases, he probably had to go through the euthanizing process where the owners chose to stay with their pets, but once they were gone, he could forgo the cost of cremation by dumping them in this pit, letting nature take its course. When someone like Kevin came along who chose not to be with his pet in their final moments, Wilkins made even more profit by skipping the euthanasia process entirely. He'd likely drag the animal up to his pit, deep in the woods where no one could hear him, put a bullet in the animal's brain and dump him in the hole. Kevin felt his legs go weak, and black spots were starting to appear before his eyes. If it weren't for his need to offer comfort to Bo, he probably would have keeled over and fallen face-first into the pile of rotting corpses.

"What the hell are you doing here? This is private property," a voice shouted from behind.

Kevin turned on wobbly legs to see Dr. Harry Wilkins standing behind him, pointing a revolver at him. Kevin was all but speechless.

"D . . . Doc . . . Wil . . . Harry. What is this? What . . ." Kevin stammered.

"What this is, Kevin, is me doing what I can to keep my business afloat. Times are tough, and I need to find ways to reduce my costs, increase my profit, and hopefully stay in business. I admit this might seem like a drastic step, but one does what one must in business. You know, the end justifies the means. If cutting a few corners and robbing a bit from Peter to pay Paul allows me to help other animals in distress, then it's something I'm willing to do."

"But . . ."

"No buts, Kevin. I do whatever I have to do, whenever I have to do it."

"But this . . . this is sick, Harry . . . once everyone in town finds out what you're doing . . . you'll be finished. You'll probably go to jail for this. It's got to be some sort of crime."

"Oh, Kevin. I wouldn't go to jail for something as minor as getting rid of a bunch of animals that were scheduled for death anyway. The most I might get is a slap on the wrist and perhaps a fine. However, if the authorities were to come up here and remove all the dead animals, they would also stumble upon the bodies of a few individuals of the human variety I have buried beneath the pile, and that might not go over so well for me."

Kevin realized his earlier imaginings might not have been as wild as he had initially thought they were. Kindly, old Doc Wilkins really was a killer. Wilkins had just confessed to murder. Kevin had no idea who Wilkins had killed or why, but now that he knew the truth, he didn't like the look of the gun in the doctor's hand. As if reading Kevin's thoughts, the doctor raised his pistol, pointing it directly at Kevin's chest, and said, "And now, Kevin, you will, unfortunately, have to join them."

Kevin heard the gun's report ring out and grabbed for his chest, sure he had been shot. Then he realized he was fine. On the other hand, the doctor was on the ground, wrestling with Bo, who had his jaws tightly wrapped around Wilkin's throat. Before Kevin could react, Bo tore the flesh away from the good doctor's throat as the man's lifeblood pumped out into the dry soil, where it immediately began to soak into the ground.

Realizing the doctor was dead, Kevin had to figure out what to do next, which was not easy in his current state of distress. If he reported the incident, the authorities would likely have no choice but to put Bo down for killing a human, and Kevin didn't think that was right. Bo was not violent by nature and had only been protecting Kevin. Wilkins was the villain in this scenario. Kevin looked around at the pit full of animals and made up his mind.

Grabbing the doctor's body by the ankles, Kevin pulled the corpse over to the edge of the pit and got ready to push it over. He felt something grab onto his ankle and saw the doctor's hand. He looked down at the man and saw Wilkins' eyes wide with fury as he tried to shout but could only manage a weak, gurgling, liquid cry. Kevin shook loose from the man's grip and pushed him into the pit. Wilkins at first landed on top of the pile of dead animals next to Duke, then the pile slowly began to shift, and Wilkins' body, still alive but barely, began to sink into the mass of creatures he, himself, had put in the pit. As his body descended, old Duke's body rolled over and landed on top of the good doctor. Kevin couldn't help but appreciate the irony in that.

Calling for Bo to follow him, Kevin headed down the trail away from the stinking pit of death and out the double gate, which now stood wide open. He saw the doctor's high-end sedan parked outside the gate with the keys still in the ignition and immediately formulated a plan. He'd come back for the doctor's car later and leave it and the keys in a disreputable part of town. It shouldn't take more than a few minutes for a car of that caliber to disappear. Since technically, the doctor was still alive when Kevin pushed him into the pit, he had more to worry about than poor Bo being put down. He was in danger of being put down himself.

Kevin closed the gates and wrapped the chain tightly around both, pulling them closed so that not even a tiny animal could squeeze through. Then he refastened the padlock and retested the gates. He used his shirt sleeve to wipe any fingerprints he might have left on the chain, gate, and lock. As he and Bo headed down the path, Kevin placed a call to Dave, telling him they were on their way and should meet outside the woods behind Dave's house.

When Dave arrived, he said, "Holly Hell, Kevin. What's all that blood doing on Bo's muzzle?"

Kevin had forgotten entirely about Bo and his bloody face. Fortunately, he thought quickly and said, "Oh . . . that . . . um . . . when

I found him, he was chomping on the carcass of a pretty good-sized rabbit. That's got to be where it came from. You can wash his face off in the backyard before you let him in the house."

"Oh, ok. Good idea," Dave said. He was so thrilled to have his dog back safely that he never questioned the blood any further.

Later that night, Kevin followed through with his plan and disposed of the doctor's car. He figured it would only be a few days before someone reported the veterinarian missing and maybe a week before someone learned about the land the doctor had owned and eventually discovered the pit.

He suspected it would make for a fascinating, if not confusing, case when authorities started sorting through the decaying bodies in the pit and not only found all those animals but found Dr. Wilkins as well as the bodies of his other victims. That was when Kevin suddenly realized something; he no longer felt sick or weak. Whatever mental problem had caused his displeasure with dealing with dead things was gone. What did they call that? Shock therapy? Perhaps immersing himself in all that death did the trick. He didn't know. All Kevin did know was he supposed he owed the doctor some thanks for whatever part the man played in his surprising recovery.

LAKELAND HOUSE OF HORRORS

To most onlookers, the nondescript building seemed in no way threatening or frightening whatsoever. It was a white wood-sided structure, faded and yellowed over years of no exterior maintenance. It had an extended roof that stretched across the building's front facade. Its mundane, box-like shape was not unlike most of the other World War II-era buildings that could be found throughout Lakeland Park. One significant difference was this building had no windows. Another more obvious difference was the ornaments that adorned the building. There were oversized black silhouettes of frightening clowns, famous movie monsters, demons, and even drama masks, the ones with happy and sad faces.

However, to eight-year-old Jimmy Kessler, the place was the scariest building on earth. The strange thing about the boy's fear was Jimmy had never been in the building. His was a case of fearing the unknown coupled with an overactive imagination, especially when it came to all things related to horror. Jimmy's discomfort with the building didn't come from its run-down appearance or even from the creepy silhouettes.

In young Jimmy Kessler's eyes, the absolute terror came from the two sets of black wooden double doors on the front of the building; one located on the far-left side and one set on the far-right side. Those doors and the iron tracks that traveled under the doors were the things that terrified him more than anything else. The place was called the Lakeland House of Horrors, and young Jimmy felt that was a fitting description indeed. He often watched those two tracks carry carloads of screaming children into the door on the left. Jimmy would watch the cars enter, their front bumpers slamming into the rubber pads on the front of the coal-black doors. That sound, that banging thud, was something that haunted Jimmy's nightmares.

It didn't matter to Jimmy that the cars always exited from the right door filled with laughing children. Jimmy only saw the double black doors being pushed open by the car, and then he would watch the car and its occupants disappear into the blackness like an animal being swallowed by some gargantuan hideous beast. As soon as the doors closed behind the cars, the screaming would begin. Jimmy had no idea what went on inside that building; all he knew was if it were even more terrifying than that initial plunge into blackness, he wanted nothing to do with the place.

"So, Jimmy. What say we give it a try?"

Jimmy looked up at his Uncle Bobby in disbelief. "Huh?" That was all he managed to squeak out.

"The ride. You know, the funhouse. How's about you and me hop into one of those cars and give it a spin. Wattaya say Sport?"

Although Jimmy hated when Uncle Bobby called him Sport, he idolized the young man nonetheless. Bobby was only seventeen, but he was like a grown man to Jimmy. He had his own car and not some old clunker, but a real cherry red hot rocking sports car. Bobby called it his chick magnet. Jimmy thought his Uncle Bobby was the coolest of the cool. After all, he dated lots of different girls, played lead guitar in a local popular rock band, and still found time today to take Jimmy to the park. This was Jimmy's fourth visit this summer, and it was only in early July.

Every time Jimmy came to the park, Uncle Bobby tried to get him to go on the haunted house ride, but Jimmy always refused. And here Bobby was asking him one again.

"I . . . I don't think so, Uncle Bobby. I don't like it."

"Don't be silly. Every time we come here, you stand outside the place, like you're doing now, and you just stare at that ride. You're not scared, are you, Jimmy?"

Jimmy was torn. Of course, he was scared and terrified beyond understanding, but he couldn't admit to his hero that he was afraid to go on the ride. From the first time he saw the run-down place, he heard the banging of those doors and the screams of the riders; he wanted no part of it. He couldn't begin to count the number of nightmares he had experienced featuring the unknown terrors that awaited behind those dreaded doors. Night after night, Jimmy's young imagination had created horrible images of the kid-eating monsters and pitchfork-wielding demons waiting for him inside that building.

"No, Uncle Bobby. I'm not scared. I just don't want to go in there, is all. I don't think I'd enjoy it."

"Sure, you would, Sport. And there's nothing whatsoever for you to worry about. You'll be sitting right next to me the whole time, and you know your Uncle Bobby would never let anything bad happen to you."

"I . . . I know that, Uncle Bobby. But . . ."

"But what? Come on, Jimmy, you know you want to do it. You're a brave kid; I know it, and I hope you know it. Besides, if you want, you can close your eyes and just open them whenever you feel comfortable."

"Jeeze, Uncle Bobby. I don't know . . ."

"Look, Jimmy. It's no big deal. It's just something you have to get past, and once you do, you'll wonder what the heck you were ever worried about. Remember when you were afraid to go near the water because you couldn't swim?"

"Yeah, I remember. You helped me not to be scared and taught me to swim. Now I can swim like a fish."

"That's right, Jimmy, and now I can help you again. This ride is nothing special. The car runs on a track by itself, and you are safe inside the car. Sure, there will be scary sounds and lights and even some crappy fake monsters that don't even look a little real. I've been on this ride a hundred times, and I can tell you it's nothing. Those Aurora monster models you like to put together are more realistic than anything you'll see in that so-called House of Horrors. I'll bet you'll spend more time laughing at the cheesy props than you'll spend being scared."

"Well . . . I guess . . . if you're sure, I'll be ok. . . ."

"OK? You'll be better than ok. The first time I went through the place, I was even younger than you. Believe me, Jimmy, by the time we're done, you'll be the master blaster of the Lakeland House Of Horrors. Here are a couple of bucks. Go over there to that ticket booth and buy us two tickets."

Jimmy took the money and, against his better judgment, bought two tickets for the haunted house. He returned and handed one to Bobby and kept the other for himself. He asked again, "Are you sure this is going to be ok, Uncle Bobby?"

Bobby smiled down at him and said, "I ga-ron-tee it."

Jimmy always laughed when Bobby said, "ga-ron-tee," but today, he was a bit too concerned to laugh, although he did manage a slight smile.

"Let's do this," Bobby said as he took Jimmy by the hand, and they walked up to the ticket-taker. The man collecting the ride tickets was a dismal-looking fellow who appeared more like a funeral director than a ticket taker. The man was rail-thin, dressed in a shabby yellowed tee shirt. He had deep-set eyes with bags and dark circles under them. He gave off a foul odor, a mix of old, unwashed sweat and yesterday's beer. The man snatched Jimmy's ticket from his hand but must have either forgotten to take Bobby's or else Jimmy didn't see him take it.

There was no one in line for the ride ahead of them, so Bobby and Jimmy could immediately take their seats in the first ride car. Jimmy began to panic, his heart thudding in his chest as the skinny man brought the safety bar down across their laps. Then the time had come. The man pulled a lever on the ride control, and the car jerked forward. Jimmy felt his heart leap into his young throat.

As the car approached the dreaded black double doors, Jimmy grabbed his Uncle Bobby's hand and gripped it as tightly as his seven-year-old fingers would permit. Bobby told him not to worry. Everything would be fine. Then, with a bang, the car entered the darkness of the Lakeland House of Horrors.

At first, Jimmy closed his eyes as tightly as possible while he listened to the shrieks, moans, and howls of the many monsters that lurked somewhere in the blackness of this horrible place. Then he noticed something; the sounds repeated. Jimmy realized those sounds weren't real monsters but were nothing more than a pre-recorded soundtrack made to scare kids and set the scary mood for the ride.

Gradually, he opened his eyes a crack, peeking through the slits of his fingers while his hands still covered his eyes. He saw many different color flashing lights and poorly done paintings of Frankenstein, Wolfman, Dracula, and The Mummy, all painted in day-glow colors. Occasionally, the car would spin in a direction, and a burst of cold air would shoot into his face, followed by a blast from a loud horn. That was scary but in a fun way.

Before he realized what was happening, Jimmy had lowered his hands from his eyes, grabbed tightly to the safety bar, and was laughing and enjoying the ride, just like Uncle Bobby said he would. Soon, Jimmy could see the light from the outside world through a crack in the exit double doors ahead, and he realized the ride was almost over. He turned to his Uncle Bobby and was about to tell him how much fun the ride was when he realized his uncle was gone. What had happened to him?

Suddenly, Jimmy's panic was back with a vengeance, and he began screaming for his uncle. Someone or something must have pulled his uncle from the car and taken him into the darkness to do what? To feast on his flesh? Somebody had planned this and distracted Jimmy with the lights and sounds so they could make off with his beloved Uncle. But how did they do it? His lap bar was still in place, and Uncle Bobby was much bigger than he was. So Bobby couldn't have been taken away. But he was gone. Terrified as never before, Jimmy began to scream and cry for his Uncle Bobby until darkness overtook him, and he passed out.

* * *

"Jimmy? Jim? Son, can you hear me?" A man's deep voice called to Jimmy in the darkness as he began to regain consciousness.

Jimmy recognized his father's voice. Why was his father calling to him? Where was Uncle Bobby?"

"Uncle . . . Bobby? Where is Uncle Bobby?" Jimmy asked weakly.

Another voice chimed in, one Jimmy recognized as the scrawny, smelly man who had collected his ticket. "I tell ya, Sir, dis kid here came on da ride alone."

Jimmy was confused and tried to say, "No . . . no . . . Daddy. Uncle Bobby was with me . . . he helped me. Where did he go?"

Jimmy's father said to the ride operator, "Look. Don't worry about it. He's awake, and he's going to be ok now. He slipped away from me earlier, and I was looking all over the park for him. I'm just glad he wasn't hurt. He's been through a lot in the past month. I'll take him home, and he'll be as good as new in a couple of days."

"Well, ok, I s'pose. Just so ya ain't gonna sue us or nothin'."

"No. No. Not to worry. You'll get no trouble from us. I just want to get my boy back home. Thanks for your assistance."

"I didn't do nothin' but call fer help. But yer welcome just the same."

Jimmy was perplexed, "Dad? Dad? Where's Uncle Bobby? He took me on the ride and made me not scared. Then he disappeared. What's going on, Daddy?"

"Don't worry, Jimmy. We'll talk about it when we get home."

Eventually, they would talk about it, and Jimmy's Dad would have to break the news to Jimmy once again carefully. His beloved Uncle Bobby had been killed in an automobile accident several weeks earlier when his cherry red sportscar wrapped itself around a telephone pole.

VACCINE

The pandemic of 2045 had been tragic beyond anyone's anticipation; so many billions of people dead, almost twenty-five percent of the world's population. There had been so much pain, suffering, and sorrow. In many ways, it made those who had survived envious of the dead. Life had drastically changed in ways no one could have ever imagined, even more so than following the COVID-19 pandemic of 2020. Like COVID and so many other pandemics before it, this virus immediately took its toll on the elderly, the weak, and the very young. Unlike previous viruses, however, this one quickly infiltrated the general population at an unprecedented rate and began claiming the lives of those individuals once considered the healthiest members of society. It took the rich, the poor, the young, the old, the weak, and the strong. No level of society was spared.

The medical name for the virus was DB-576/843, but that name quickly became irrelevant when the media came up with the nickname the "Gray Death." This name arose from the appearance of the pandemic victims. The virus destroyed the body's ability to absorb oxygen, essentially suffocating its victims from the inside out. This left a corpse whose flesh had turned a dusky blue-gray color.

The plague was merciless. Virtually everyone, everywhere in the world, had lost someone close to them. Entire families were destroyed. As if the virus had not done enough damage itself, millions of people committed suicide, choosing to be the instrument of their demise rather than fall victim to the Gray Death. It seemed as if no one was spared the touch of this dreaded plague. Neither quarantines nor social distancing nor any of the other proven CDC-recommended protocols did anything to stop the spread of the Gray Death.

Eventually, scientists were able to develop a vaccine for the virus. Using lessons learned from the COVID-19 pandemic and others before it, the world's governments were able to ramp up vaccine production quickly, set up distribution channels, and eventually establish vaccination centers. However, because of the desperate need for a vaccine, many traditional testing protocols had to be bypassed. The result was a vaccine that worked very well . . . that is to say when it worked. When it didn't, the results were unpredictable and often tragic.

In the case of some people who had reactions to the vaccine, some side effects became evident immediately, while others showed up in the days or weeks to follow. Some of the adverse reactions were as simple as headaches, fever, and body aches. However, others were much more severe, producing side effects like respiratory and kidney failures, usually resulting in death. Most of the information permitted to be released to the public was regarding those few less severe symptoms that occurred in the first few minutes or overnight. The government thought it best not to mention any long-term ill effects. It would be more than a decade before those incidents were made public, including the staggering number of birth defects that rivaled those of the Thalidomide tragedy of the mid-twentieth century resulting from mothers who had gotten the vaccine while in the early stages of pregnancy.

However, when one had to choose between the risk of having a potentially lethal reaction to an unproven vaccine or succumbing to the Gray Death, what might have once been considered a roll of the dice suddenly became much more straightforward.

Before the Gray Death, Sean Montgomery had been a senior engineer for a local aerospace components manufacturer. He was no stranger to the protocols put into place to help fight off pandemics. During the COVID-19 pandemic, Sean was in his late twenties. He had been working for a company in a capacity that was determined to be essential. So, when the Governor of Pennsylvania at that time, Tom

Wolf, took steps to shut down all non-essential businesses and employees, Sean was able to keep working during the whole almost two-year span of the pandemic. Now, twenty-five years later, he found himself in a similar situation. He was still essential as far as the government was concerned, but he wished he were not.

He had managed to accrue a substantial nest egg, and for the first time in his career, he could afford to be laid off for a while. He was divorced with no children, so his expenses were minimal. Unlike the COVID pandemic of 2020, the chances of contracting the Gray Death were much more likely, and its results were much more likely to be fatal. His employer, realizing how critical his essential employees were, doubled their pay during this period. Even at that, several of Sean's co-workers quit their jobs, refusing to leave their homes. If someone were to ask Sean why he was willing to take on such a risk, he would have told them the money was good, but that wasn't his motivation.

The truth was he had a strong work ethic, and the idea of abandoning his position at such a critical time in history was something he just couldn't do. If his employer went out of business or chose to eliminate his job, that would have been a different situation, one beyond his control. However, he knew that would not likely happen in the best of conditions, and now, with the world in such a terrible situation, it was impossible. So, Sean continued to report to work every day, wearing all the PPE (Protective Personal Equipment) necessary to help reduce his potential exposure to the deadly virus.

Sean feared if he didn't get the vaccine soon, he might not survive this pandemic. Unfortunately, he was far down on the list of anyone being considered for the new vaccine. He was only fifty-six years old and in good physical condition. The vaccine was presently in Phase 1, which meant only people over 65 years old or people with chronic medical conditions, compromised immune systems, diabetes, or obesity were eligible for the vaccine. It would likely be Phase 3 or 4 before they finally got to Sean.

He worried he might not make it that long. Although his concerns were justified, the worldwide panic spread by the various forms of news outlets and postings on social media had put the entire world in a state of frenzy. No one knew what to believe, how much of what they saw was real, and how much was an exaggeration. However, few could dispute the reality of the current mortality rate climbing daily.

One morning, Sean sat at his kitchen table before work, eating breakfast, and turned on the local news broadcast. A tired-looking news reporter, wearing a surgical facemask, was standing in front of the city hospital, apparently making some important announcement. Sean turned up the volume.

". . . and Governor Jackson guaranteed more than twenty thousand vaccines will be given in the next two weeks to those who have been determined to be in essential jobs. It is recommended that anyone who feels they qualify should contact their employer's personnel office as quickly as possible to get on the list for potential vaccination. As has been the tradition since the development of the vaccine, the government will use a lottery to determine who will receive the vaccine."

At first, Sean was excited at the potential of receiving the vaccine as he was among those considered essential. Then he remembered the lottery. Sure, he could get on the list of essential workers, but that didn't guarantee he'd get the vaccine. It would all be the luck of the draw. When it came to participating in games of chance, Sean never won. So, a week later, when the certified letter arrived telling him his number had been picked and he was eligible for vaccination, he was blown away. The letter also provided him with a phone number to call to schedule his injection.

He didn't care where he had to go or what time he had to be there; he was going to be there. If he had to schedule a vacation day or even two and drive 500 miles, he would do whatever he had to do to get that vaccine. After he called to set up his appointment, Sean was surprised to learn how easy it was to arrange to get his shot, which he did immediately.

A week later, he arrived at his designated time at the inoculation facility. The location was a former laboratory/research and development facility for a battery company that was no longer utilized. A large step van bearing the Center for Disease Control logo was parked outside the facility. Sean knew very well why the van was there, and it caused a knot to form in the pit of his stomach. He did his best to put the memory out of his mind.

He was suddenly filled with mixed emotions. He was happy to be finally getting his vaccine, yet he was depressed at being reminded about the havoc the Gray Death had reeked upon the world. He was also having a bit of anxiety, wondering if he would be one of the rare unfortunates who had adverse reactions to the vaccine. He felt as if he were being pulled in multiple directions simultaneously.

He stopped for a moment, looking up at the glass facade of the building, seeing the line of people inside waiting to be vaccinated, as well as the volunteers registering them. Then, he realized his fears were not justified. The number of people who had died from the vaccine was minimal. Less than a tenth of one percent of vaccinated died, whereas millions of unvaccinated had already succumbed to the virus. Being an essential worker who had to go out among the great unwashed every day, Sean knew his chances of contracting the Gray Death were much greater than most.

This thought helped dispel his temporary uncertainty, so Sean opened the door and entered the vaccination center. He immediately encountered a large white sign with red letters mounted on a pole reading, "Be sure to wear a mask and please maintain a minimum of six feet distance away from the other people in line. This facility follows mandatory CDC guidelines for social distancing."

Sean already had his mask in place as he never left his house without one. He wore two masks all the time for double protection. He figured he could never be too safe. He counted the people in line ahead of him and was pleased to see only about ten of them. The line seemed longer because of their socially distant spacing. As he waited, a volunteer in a hazmat suit walked up along the line with a portable scanning device and a handheld temperature scanner. The first scanner was a barcode reader. Sean presented his smartphone, which displayed a square QR code for the scanner to read. It contained all his pertinent medical information, including his authorization to be there.

The second scanner was to measure his temperature. Had his temperature been above 101 degrees, it would indicate that he might have unknowingly contracted the virus, and isolation protocols would be immediately put into place. However, Sean felt fine. He was confident he had no fever, yet the thought of having his temperature checked made his palms suddenly feel clammy.

That memory he had barely managed to suppress earlier when he saw the CDC truck now came screaming to the surface. Sean had seen what happened when the workers encountered someone with a high temperature, and it was not a pleasant experience to live through. He recalled how a month earlier, he had been standing in a line outside of his place of employment, socially distanced, of course, waiting to have his temperature verified and be admitted into his office. He saw one of his co-workers at the front of the line, having his temperature taken. Although this was a daily requirement for all essential workers, and although he knew it was a necessary precaution, Sean felt it was a bit demeaning, if not Orwellian. Bob Edmunds, a fellow engineer who worked in a cubical two or three units away from Sean's, was the person he saw at the front of the line.

The company nurse looked at the reading on the scanner, shook it, and took Bob's temperature a second time. She shouted, "101," and then panic ensued. The people in line behind Bob broke ranks and ran back out into the parking lot, practically knocking Sean to the ground, so much for social distancing. When Sean regained his footing, he saw Bob sitting in a wooden chair, staring down at his feet, looking like he had just lost his best friend. The company nurse was on her smartphone, speaking with someone and keeping her distance from him. Bob raised his head and locked eyes with Sean. If he lived to be a hundred, Sean knew he would never forget how Bob Edmunds' eyes changed within seconds, running the emotional gamut from confusion, fear, anger, understanding, and finally to sad acceptance.

Moments later, a medical van with the logo for the CDC came screeching to a stop in front of the office, followed by a police squad car. A team of government healthcare workers burst from the CDC van and made their way through the front door, heading directly for Bob. They put him into a disposable yellow suit like their clothes, then led Bob past Sean and out the door. Bob was unceremoniously loaded into the CDC vehicle, and the double doors were slammed shut. With sirens screaming, the team drove away. Another unit arrived moments later and began scrubbing down the area. After that day, Sean never saw Bob again. A few weeks later, he learned Bob had succumbed to the Gray Death.

Now, as he stood in line waiting, a nurse was using a digital temperature scanner, almost identical to the one that sealed Bob Edmund's fate, to determine his fate. As she approached Sean, she placed the tip of the scanner near the side of his neck and pulled the trigger. Sean had never seen a scanner used in this fashion. His temperature had always been taken on his forehead. What was with this neck thing?

Sean felt like time had slowed to an agonizing crawl as he watched the nurse's face for any tell-tale expressions. He was certain any second, she would shout out some unacceptable temperature number. Then, a group of medical professionals would swarm down on him and drag him into the CDC van outside. It would speed him away, and no one would ever see Sean Wilson Montgomery again.

To his relief, the nurse smiled, indicating his temperature must have been within the acceptable range. She directed Sean to the following table, where he presented his medical insurance card and driver's license to verify his identity.

The volunteer sitting at the opposite side of the table smiled and said, "Good morning, Sean. I'm Bob. We're so happy you came to be vaccinated today. I know this isn't the most pleasant way to spend your morning, but I'll do everything I can to make your time with us as worry-free as possible."

Sean was caught off guard for a moment and said, "Thanks, um . . . Bob, nice to meet you." They, of course, did not shake hands. No one shook hands these days. Hardly anyone has shaken hands since the last pandemic of 2020. There had been a myriad of attempts over the years to come up with a more acceptable, safer way of greeting. During the COVID-19 pandemic, the elbow bump started to take hold as a possible substitution for shaking hands. The problem was many people felt that the greeting looked ridiculous. In addition, being the first attempt at a greeting substitute, it served to constantly remind people of the pandemic they were living through, as if continually wearing face masks was not reminder enough. In addition, several other new forms of greetings had begun to emerge, none of which had taken hold, so the greeter could never be sure which one to use.

Then there had been the less safe but also less ridiculous-looking fist bump. Many people were opposed to any skin-to-skin contact, so that one didn't last very long. Some folks tried to popularize a greeting where you pointed at your heart and then at the person you were greeting, but that seemed too much like something from a bad sci-fi movie, and it never gained footing, either. In the end, most people settled for just a head nod with an uncomfortable smile. The discomfort came from the constant reminder that germs were so quickly spread. At least it was painful for the generations that grew up with strong handshakes and bro hugs. Sean suspected that for the generations to follow, the lack of physical contact would be as typical for them as it was now strange for him. That thought only served to depress him further.

Sean was surprised that the volunteer across the table had introduced himself in such a friendly manner. He assumed that must be part of the training protocol the volunteer was given to lower the vaccine recipient's stress level.

Sean thought, *OK. Bob, old boy. At the risk of seeming rude, the truth is, I couldn't care less what your name is, and you can stop grinning at me any time now. All I want is to get this stinking vaccine over with so I can go on with my life.*

Smiling, Bob—as Sean now thought of him—directed Sean to fill out paperwork, which included a hold harmless agreement protecting both the volunteers and the vaccine manufacturers from any litigation due to the potential side effects or complications from the injection, including death. This did little to make Sean feel warm and fuzzy, yet what choice did he have? People were dropping like flies out there in the real world. At least, this vaccine had the potential of offering him protection against the virus, that was, assuming it didn't cause a third eye to appear in the middle of his forehead.

Sean glanced up at Smiling Bob, and for the briefest of moments, something impossible occurred. Bob's face seemed to change. It was as if there was another liquid face swimming just beneath the man's regular face. It appeared to be a horrid, deformed, rotting skull-like version of Smiling Bob's face. It was teeming with maggots that wiggled and crawled underneath the decomposing flesh. Sean's breath caught in his throat, and he gave an involuntary gasp.

"Are you ok, Sean?" Smiling, Bob asked, his face now returned to its regular jovial expression.

Sean stammered, "Um . . . ah . . . yes, yes, sorry. Must be . . . you know, nerves."

Bob said, "I'm sure that's all it is, Sean. Believe me, everything will be fine. Now, if you would just sign these papers, we can get you on your way. I don't mean to rush you, but we have a lot of eager folks waiting behind you. Sean looked around at the long line starting to snake outside around the building and turned back to Bob, half expecting to see the horror return, but it did not. Sean signed the documents, and Smiling Bob directed him to a hallway leading to the vaccination area. It was a surprisingly poorly lit hall, which felt more like a tunnel than a hallway, but fortunately, it wasn't very long, and in a few steps, Sean could see the light ahead.

Light at the end of the tunnel, Sean thought, and then he remembered the old worn-out joke, *Hopefully, it's not a train coming to run me down.* Sean knew it was a strange thought and blamed it too on his nervousness. *Calm down, Sean, old boy. Smiling Bob told you everything will be fine.* Then Sean wondered why he should believe anyone who had a maggot-infested rotting face under his outer face. Then he asked himself if he had really seen what he had thought he saw or that, or was it simply a trick of his over-stressed imagination?

As Sean left the hall and entered the brightly lit vaccination room, he was greeted by yet another volunteer. She took Sean's registration card, read it, and said with a smile, "Good morning, Sean, my name is Ginger."

He looked at Ginger and saw an elderly woman in a floral-patterned smock and medical scrubs with a prominently displayed smiley face sticker reading "Ginger" written in pink marker. She looked like everyone's beloved grandmother.

"Good morning, Ginger," he said as he looked around the room. It was a large area, the size of a gymnasium, but with a lower ceiling, perhaps ten feet high. The room was brightly illuminated with fluorescent overhead lighting. It appeared to have been a testing laboratory at some point, judging by the strategically spaced electric receptacles all around the room's perimeter, on the ceiling and embedded in the hardwood flooring. Sean could easily have imagined the room filled with rows of worktables covered in electronic gadgetry such as oscilloscopes and the like. Now, it was essentially a massive space filled with dozens of temporary folding tables.

Each table had a folding chair positioned on either side and a volunteer standing near the middle of the table. There were boxes stacked on the tables. Sean assumed some contained the vaccine and others had general medical supplies, such as alcohol to swab the injection area, gauze, and adhesive bandages to cover the injection site. There was also a red box with the biohazard label prominently displayed. That was where they discarded the used syringes.

"Please head down there to table 27," Ginger said from Sean's right.

He turned and saw her pointing an index finger toward the front of the room. At first, her outstretched arm looked as normal as anyone's, but then, like Smiling Bob's face, Ginger's hand began to change. The flesh at first became bright red then the skin started to bubble. Pustules expanded like melting cheese on a pizza in an oven and then exploded. They shot out a volcanic eruption of greenish-yellow ooze, which drizzled down the woman's flesh like molten lava, digging furrows in her skin and causing sections of meat to slough off and drip like tallow to the floor, leaving an exposed, pointing skeletal hand in its wake.

"Are you alright, Sean?" Volunteer Ginger inquired with caution. She was staring at Sean with astonished concern as if he were about to pass out or have some other medical problem. The woman's hideous hand had returned to normal. "Down there at the front of the room. That's table 27."

Sean saw a table with a large sign taped to the front reading 27.

"T . . . t . . . thank y . . . y . . . you," Sean stuttered as he started walking toward the designated table. His legs were beginning to feel wobbly, and he had no idea what was happening to him or why he was seeing the strange things he was seeing. He was neither psychic nor clairvoyant and had never experienced such hallucinations before. He took a deep breath and headed toward table number 27.

He realized he hadn't noticed the numbers on the tables before, but now, as Sean glanced around, he saw there were more than forty numbered tables, each identical to the other. As he approached table 27, he saw his volunteer standing, waiting for him to take a seat. The volunteer was a thin, pale young man in his mid-thirties with a receding hairline of light brown and that same strange, Cheshire cat smile that Smiling Bob had worn. The smiling man reached out his hand and took Sean's identification card, which Ginger had returned to him.

The man looked at the card and said, "Good morning, Sean. I'm Gary. We're so happy you came to be vaccinated today. I know this isn't the most pleasant way to spend your morning, but I'll do everything I can to make your time with us as worry-free as possible," Gary grinned at Sean, sending a chill down his spine.

Sean thought, *Didn't he just say the same thing Smiling Bob said to me? Training or not, that's weird.* He found it all of this way too creepy.

Sean said, "Um . . . thanks, Gary. If it's all the same to you, I'd like to get this over with as soon as possible."

"I understand completely," Gary said with a "we strive for excellent customer service" grin that made Sean cringe.

Then it happened again. Grinning Gary's face began to morph into something resembling a death's head, every bit as gruesome, if not more so, than Smiling Bob's had been. The maggots were back, along with gray worm-like creatures that were crawling out of the specter's empty eye sockets. Sean looked away for a second, and when he looked back, Gary's regular face had returned.

"Is everything ok, Sean?" Grinning Gary asked, apparently as concerned as the other volunteers appeared to be.

"Um . . . uh . . . yeah . . . yes, I'm fine. Just a bit nervous, is all."

As he uncapped a pre-filled syringe of the vaccine, Gary said, "Well then, Sean, let's get this over with and get you on your way. If you will be so kind as to roll up your sleeve and expose your arm up to your shoulder, we'll get this bit of unpleasant business out of the way. Also, you may have noticed a series of chairs at the back of the room where you entered. We require that you stay for fifteen minutes after your injection."

"Why is that?" Sean said as he rolled up his tee-shirt sleeve, exposing his upper arm. He didn't want to stay here any longer than he had to. The place was freaking him out.

"Just protocol. You know, just a precaution," Gary said with his trademark grin.

"Precaution?" Sean felt his chest tighten slightly.

"Yes. Just a safety precaution. You see, most people experience little or no side effects from the vaccine, but those rare few who do tend to have their reaction within the first fifteen minutes. So just as a precaution, we have people wait around for a bit."

Sean felt sweat begin to trickle down the center of his back. He asked, "Have you witnessed any of those reactions?"

"Um . . . well, Sean. No, not really. I did have one person who got nauseous, but to be honest, I believe that was more the result of nerves rather than the vaccine. If it helps any, I've gotten the vaccine myself, and other than a sore arm, I had no problems. If you've ever had a flu shot, it's a lot like that."

"Ok then, let's rock and roll," Sean said, sounding less confident than he would have liked.

Gary inserted the inch-long needle into Sean's upper arm and injected the clear fluid into his muscle. Sean expected to feel heat streaking up and down his arm and experience agonizing pain suddenly but felt nothing but the pinch of the needle.

"All done," grinning, Gary said, "now, if you'll go back and take a seat for fifteen minutes, you'll be good to go. Take care, Sean."

"Thanks," Sean said uncomfortably as he rose and headed back to the bank of chairs at the rear of the room. As he walked, he saw dozens of people going through the same process he had just completed and heard random bits of conversations along the way, the volunteers all stating their names and repeating the scripted greetings he had already heard twice. He decided to keep his eyes focused forward less he saw more of those strange hallucinations he had seen earlier. He figured if his problem was caused by nervous tension, it should go away as soon as the worst was over. The shot was done, the vaccine administered, and in fifteen minutes, he would put this place and all its weirdness in his rearview mirror.

He took a seat and saw a large round analog clock hanging nearby on a wall near the door where he had entered and met Granny Ginger. She was busy with the latest person to come through the door. The time on the wall clock was 8:35. Sean took out his smartphone and confirmed the time, happy to see that both clocks agreed. Then, he took a few minutes to look for any important messages or missed calls, scan his email, and check out social media for any posts of interest. When he figured a few minutes had passed, he put his phone away and looked over at the clock on the wall. It still read 8:35.

Perplexed, he took out his smartphone again and saw that it also said 8:35. But how was that possible? He was sure he had spent a good six or seven minutes on his phone, yet both clocks seemed to have remained unchanged. He looked over at the wall clock again and saw it had still not yet changed.

Then he glanced at the doorway next to the clock, the one he had entered through earlier, and saw a man standing there. The man seemed to be looking right at Sean. However, that was not the strangest element of this encounter. The man looked exactly like his father. A cold chill ran down Sean's spine again as he stared back at his dad's doppelganger. Who was this guy? Could his father have had a relative of whom Sean was unaware? To the best of his knowledge, all of Sean's uncles were dead, and none of his cousins looked like his father. Sean's dad had passed away more than two decades earlier, and although he thought of him daily, Sean had never encountered anyone who had ever looked so much like him before. And why was the guy staring at him with that strange smile?

Sean rose from his chair and started toward the door without thinking about it. He was going to get to the bottom of this. It was possible that once he got closer to the guy, he would see that the resemblance had all been imagined, and the stranger probably didn't look anything like his dad. His imagination was obviously operating with all cylinders firing today, so he supposed anything was possible. As he walked toward the doorway, Sean saw the man's eyes never shift away from his own. To make matters worse, the closer he got, the more the man resembled his late father.

When he reached the doorway, the man finally looked away from Sean, back toward the bank of chairs Sean had left behind. Then, the man raised his hand and pointed silently in that direction. Sean slowly turned around, already suspecting what he would see there. He felt someone grasping his hand, while at the same time, he saw his own body sprawled out on the floor next to his chair. The body spasmed and twitched several times before going still. His smartphone was still clutched in the claw-like grip of his hand. Several volunteers had begun to surround his body, staring down helplessly at his now cooling corpse. Several people had jumped up out of their chairs and were staring down at his body. Some looked on in shocked horror, some were crying, and still, others were heartlessly taking video of the incident with their smartphones.

Sean felt a tug on his hand as his father, his real father, not some look-alike, led him out through the doorway and down the hallway. It was no longer dark and dismal but was brightly lit with an even brighter light waiting at the end.

THAT'S ENTERTAINMENT

"So, what are ya in for?" The rail-thin man asked, his body appearing to swim in his government-issued recyclable jumpsuit. He sat on the edge of a metal cot in the corner of the jail cell. His head hung down, and his cuffed hands dangled loosely between his legs. His feet were secured with chained manacles. The man didn't even bother to lift his head or make eye contact with the other man who had just shuffled into the cell, equally bound in shackles and cuffs. He didn't care who this character was or what crime he had committed. He was just trying to be social, you know, initiating a little small talk. Whoever this loser might happen to be was of no concern to Jackie Mack. This was Jackie's first cellmate since he had been unceremoniously dumped in the place two hours earlier. If things got rolling soon the way he suspected they would and always did, his new roomie would be just another fading memory among so many others before him.

This new arrival was dressed in a matching jumpsuit made of the same paper-ish biodegradable crap that Jackie wore, but even using his peripheral vision, he could see the guy was of a decent build. Not big, not overly muscular, just decent. Jackie had tried everything over the past several years to build himself up, but it was all to no avail. He was the original ninety-eight-pound weakling; at least, that was how he appeared. Although looks were most definitely deceiving in his case. In truth, Jackie was quite strong with ropey, sinewy muscles. However, his true gifts were his speed, cunning, responsiveness, and ability to do whatever he needed to be done with a complete lack of conscience or remorse. Jackie Mack was not someone to underestimate; he was one dangerous human being.

The new arrival said, "Huh? What did you say?"

Jackie tried to appear disinterested and repeated, "I asked what ya were in here for. Ya know? Like, what bit of heinous malfeasance did you perpetrate?"

The man did not respond. He was eyeballing Jackie intently as if weighing the situation, unsure of how to proceed. Perhaps he didn't understand what Jackie had just said. Jackie ventured a glance at the man, and he did have a look of confusion on his round, beard-stubbled young face.

Jackie shook his head and returned to staring down at the floor. He said, Look. Maybe that was too personal a question for ya. Here's an easier one. I'm Jackie. Jackie Mack. What's yer name?"

The man remained warily uncertain for a few seconds, then stammered, "Ar . . . arm . . . Armed robbery."

Jackie smiled that unique crooked smile he reserved for moments when he decided to share his talent for sarcasm and said, "That's one Hell of an unusual name ya got there, Armed. Or maybe I should call ya Mr. Robbery?"

The man hesitated for a second, then upon realizing his mistake, he corrected, "No, no. Sorry. My name is Charlie, Charlie Danvers. My crime was armed robbery."

"Oh, ok. I see. A little slow on the uptake, are we? If I may be so presumptuous to inquire . . . why in the name of all that is sane would anyone rob any liquor store, bank, pawnshop, mini-mart, or, for that matter, anywhere that had cameras recording every time ya scratched your nuts? Ya see, my new friend, unless you've spent the last decade on an Amish farm or in a cave with Bigfoot, ya might have noticed cameras are everywhere."

Charlie said, "I . . . um . . . I suppose I hadn't been paying attention. I was . . . you know, desperate. I've been out of work for about two years, and I needed the money for my family, wife, and three kids. You know? I guess . . . I guess I didn't realize the place would have cameras."

"Oh, Charles, Charles, my poor unknowing fool. There are cameras everywhere, watching our every move 24-7. There are even cameras in here." Jackie jerked his head in the direction of the corner of the cell near the ceiling.

Charlie looked up and saw a camera lens mounted on a metal arm, slowly panning back and forth. Then he looked outside the cell and saw several others positioned strategically down the length of the hallway of cells.

"Why are there cameras here? It's not like we can escape or anything. They got us cuffed and shackled." Charlie rattled his writs, then tried to pull on the thick bars of the cell door. They didn't budge a bit or rattle like they often did in old television westerns.

Jackie said, "They want to make sure we're alive and well. Ya know. They want to be sure we don't do anything to hurt ourselves or each other."

Charlie looked a bit concerned, and Jackie could sense the man tightening up his muscles as if preparing to be assaulted. "I don't have to worry about that with you, do I, Jackie? I don't want no trouble, ok?"

Jackie chuckled and said, "Not to worry, Charlie, my friend. You'll get no trouble from me in here. I'm just sitting here doing nothing. The only thing I'm killing at the moment is time."

"Good. That's good to hear. Cause I may look a bit soft, but I can handle myself if I need to."

"Color me impressed," Jackie said, allowing more of his sarcasm to slip in.

Jackie could see Charlie was starting to relax, getting more comfortable with the situation. Then Charlie asked, "So Jackie. I told you what I did. What are you in here for?"

Jackie sneered and said, "Well, I can guaran-damn-tee ya it wasn't for robbing no convenience store."

"Ok. Ok. I get your point. So, what did you do?"

"I killed a cop."

"You what? Did you say you killed a cop?"

"Yeah, I suppose I did."

"And you think I'm an idiot for robbing a store. You killed a cop? Holy Hell, Jackie. That makes me look like a genius. You know what they do to cop killers?"

"Yep, I do. I know very well. I've spent the last several years knowing," Jackie replied.

Charlie started walking back and forth nervously in the cell, mumbling, "Jesus, Mary, and Joseph! I can't believe it. All I did was rob a stupid store, and they put me in a cell with a murderer. And a cop killer, no less."

Jackie said, "Chill, Charlie. It's all good. It's not like I'm going to jump up and try to strangle ya or anything. What I did, I did a long, long time ago. And believe it or not, I wasn't a murderer by nature. It was just a bit of an unfortunate set of circumstances I don't particularly care to discuss that led to my present sad situation."

"That's quite alright. Don't tell me. I don't think I want to know anyway. I just want to get out of here." Charlie was becoming increasingly agitated.

"Not to worry, Charlie, my friend. We won't be in here long. We never are."

"Don't call me your friend. You don't know me, and I don't want to know more about you. And what do you mean we won't be in here long?"

Jackie smiled his sly smile and said, "Ya mean you don't know?"

"Don't know what?" Charlie asked, confused.

"I mean, ya don't know why we're here and what's going to happen next?"

Charlie said, "No, of course not. I've never been convicted of a crime before and never been in jail. I have no idea what you're talking about. Up until I had to rob that store, I was what most folks would consider a model citizen."

Jackie asked, "Don't ya follow sports? Ain't ya never heard of the big game?"

"No, no, I haven't heard of any big game. I've been too busy trying to survive. I haven't had a TV or a computer for well over two years."

"My oh my. This is going to be good," Jackie said.

"What do you mean?"

"What I mean is, much can change in a year or so, Charlie. Governments can be replaced. People's needs can change. Hell, the entire moral structure of a nation can flip-flop practically overnight. And the way a country deals with its so-called criminal element can change as well."

"What the Hell is that supposed to mean?"

"It means, Charlie, that you've been out of touch for a while, but time has chosen to march steadily onward, leaving ya back in its dust."

Charlie appeared even more confused, "And . . . ?"

Jackie looked past Charlie at the dozen guards making their way up along the hallway of jail cells, opening each door and systematically removing the prisoners. They were leading them down the darkened hallway, away from their cells. Two monstrously large guards opened the door to their cell, looked down at their clipboards, and one of them said, "Charles Danvers?"

"Um . . . yes, I'm Charlie Danvers."

"Of course you are," one angry-looking guard said. Then they looked at Jackie and said, "And, of course, we know you very well. Don't we, Jackie?" the guard asked.

"Hey, Bob. Hey George. Good to see you again."

"Just shut your stinkin' pie hole, cop-killer," George grumbled.

Bob said, "Now, George. There's no need to get hostile. Jackie's made a lot of people a boatload of money betting on the big game. Isn't that right, Jackie?"

Jackie said, "I suppose it is. And hopefully, I'll be making ya more today. That is if ya played your cards right." He looked knowingly at the guard named George.

Bob replied, "Not to worry, Jackie. I've played them as I always do. Right as rain."

George stared angrily back at Jackie and interrupted, "I didn't cop-killer. And maybe today it will be my turn to win big."

Jackie shook his head and said, "Oh, poor George. Ya never learn, do ya? How much have ya lost betting against me? Hundreds? Thousands?"

George snarled, "It don't matter. It don't matter one lousy bit, you hear? I'd lose every penny I had before I bet on you. You cop-killing bastard!"

Bob said, "Now that'll be enough of that, George. Let's get these two moving."

Charlie was more confused than ever. He asked, "Moving? Where are you taking us? What's this all about?"

Bob looked at Jackie perplexed and asked, "Jackie? Is this guy serious? He really doesn't know?"

"Nope. He's apparently been living under a rock for the past year or so. He is completely oblivious."

Bob smiled and said, "Oh boy. This is going to be great."

"That's pretty much what I said," Jackie replied with a sly smile.

The two guards led the shackled convicts down the dimly lit corridor, eventually catching up with the other guards and prisoners. Charlie didn't like this one bit. He could see the other convicts shuffling along in front of him, walking with their heads hung down, looking like they were going to their execution. He thought he heard a few of them weeping. One man was mumbling almost incoherently. It sounded like he was saying, "It's not right. You can't do this in our country. I have rights."

Charlie heard a guard say, "Shut up, sissy boy," followed by the thumping sound of flesh against flesh. He heard a whimper then the mumbling fell silent.

"What the Hell is going on here, Jackie? I don't like this."

Bob chuckled and said, "Relax, Danvers. We're going to the big game."

"The big game? What's that?"

George laughed and said, "Wow, cop-killer, your buddy here really has been living under a rock, holey crow."

"Yeah, well, we all know that's all about to change very shortly," Jackie said with little emotion in his voice. The time for that was over. Now, it was time to do what must be done.

Suddenly, two large wooden doors were pushed open, flooding the dark tunnel with blinding light. Charlie put his hands up to shield his eyes, and through his squinting, he could see glimpses and flashes of movement around him. He heard the roar of what sounded like several thousand people cheering and madly stomping their feet. He saw all his fellow prisoners trying to run out into the light, although the best they could manage was a clumsy, shambling gait. He felt Jackie coming up alongside him. Charlie tried to call out to him, but Jackie shoved him against the stone wall as he hurried past. Charlie bumped his head against the wall, saw stars, and for a moment, he thought he was going to pass out.

He shook off the feeling and heard the roaring crowd screaming even louder. Now that his eyes had adjusted to the light and his head had begun to clear, Charlie couldn't believe his eyes. All the prisoners picked various weapons from a huge pile in the center of a gigantic arena. At first, he thought it might be an escape attempt; then, he saw the inmates were fighting and killing each other. The roar of the crowd was deafening. There were half a dozen cameras on booms and platforms filming the slaughter, which was simultaneously being projected onto three massive digital video screens. He saw families in the crowd, some with small children. He saw food and snack vendors walking among the incredible crowd. He could smell popcorn, hot dogs, beer, and something else. He could smell the coppery scent of blood and the stench of defecation.

Charlie looked out and saw several inmates lying on the ground, their screams of agony silenced by the din of the audience. Their intestines were spilled onto the gravel floor of the arena, leaking blood and waste onto the sodden stones. Many of the inmates were still fighting like animals—those with weapons slashing, those without punching and clawing, fighting to stay alive. Charlie was staring at the spectacle, stunned almost to the point of paralysis, when someone pushed him from behind, sending him stumbling out into the melee. That was what this gorefest was: a primitive, savage melee. The crowd was eating it up, screaming louder with savage bloodlust.

The crowd started shouting a name. At first, it was faint and barely recognizable. Then, as the cries got louder, Charlie recognized who they were cheering for. The audience screamed, "Jackie, Jackie,

Jackie. Over and over, they chanted; they shouted with fervor the likes of which Charlie had never heard before. Then he recalled how the guard, Bob, had talked about making money off Jackie, and the guard, George, had lost money betting against Jackie. Was this the big game they were talking about? A dozen or so chained and manacled convicts murdering each other for the pleasure of thousands of sick individuals? Then he remembered the TV cameras. That meant millions could be watching this butchery.

What had happened to the world in the past two years? How was it that he didn't know about this? It seemed impossible, yet here it was. And what about him? What was going to happen to him? Charlie felt someone shove him from behind again, and he fell to the stone ground, feeling the knees of his paper suit rip open along with his flesh. He was now crawling on his hands and bloody knees. He looked up and saw Jackie shuffling toward him, his manacles rattling.

Jackie's paper jumpsuit was in tatters and soaked crimson with gore. He held a long sword in his right hand as he approached Charlie. His eyes looked cold and hungry, like those of a wild animal. The crowd was cheering even more loudly, "Jackie! Jackie! Jackie!"

As Jackie got closer, Charlie asked him, "Oh my God, Jackie. What is this."

Jackie smiled and said, "It's nothing personal, Charlie, my man. It's just what we have to do."

With that, Charlie saw Jacky raise his blood-splattered sword. It glimmered in the stadium lights as it swung downward. One second later, the blade cleanly severed Charlie's head, and it dropped unceremoniously onto the stones. Charlie's body remained prone for a few seconds longer, blood pumping from its neck stump before it collapsed in a heap to the ground.

George said, "Dammit, Bob, it looks like your cop-killing buddy did it again. I lost my shirt again, and I suppose you won a bundle. It just ain't fair."

Bob said, "Maybe not fair, George, but that's entertainment!"

CHILDREN OF THE NIGHT

"Deep into that darkness peering, long I stood there,
wondering, fearing, doubting, dreaming dreams
no mortal ever dared to dream before."
—Edgar Allan Poe

"Stare at the dark too long and you will eventually
see what isn't there."
—Unknown

"Listen to them, the children of the night.
What music they make!"
—Bram Stoker (Dracula)

"There are horrors beyond life's edge that we do not suspect, and
once in a while man's evil prying calls them just within our range."
—H. P. Lovecraft

It was 5:15 on a chilly April Pennsylvania morning. Daylight savings
time had just kicked in a few weeks earlier. It was still pitch-black
outside, save for the minimal illumination from the sliver of a moon
above. Usually, Paul could hear a few morning birds chirping in the
darkness as he stood in his kitchen, getting ready to head out to work.
But not this morning; today, there was not a single sound.

He happened to glance over at the bow window he had recently
installed at his kitchen eating area and saw something glowing out on

his covered patio. Paul watched it through a slight separation in the Roman shades that hung from each of the three windows. He recognized the glow immediately from the new combination digital clock and thermometer, which he had hung on one of his patio roof's wide wooden support posts. From where he stood, he couldn't read either the time or the temperature. However, this was no problem as he had just checked the time on his kitchen microwave oven and the temperature on his smartphone. It was only 28 degrees, cold for a morning in April indeed.

Nonetheless, Paul found himself almost transfixed by the strange blue and white eerie glow of the unit's screen. Although it was nothing but a ghostly light from his vantage point, Paul couldn't help but find it so incredibly captivating. He had awakened more than forty minutes earlier, showered and dressed for work, yet the remnants of his evening's sleep still clung insistently to him. Perhaps that was why he had trouble pulling his eyes away from the glow.

As he stared at the display, something odd happened. For a fraction of a second, the glow went black. It wasn't like there was a power glitch, but something had passed between his field of vision and the unit, something moving from left to right. But that was impossible. There could be no one out on his patio. Someone would have to pass through his yard to get to his patio, which was a veritable gauntlet of motion-sensitive LED lights, each one bright enough to turn night into day.

Paul took out his smartphone again, but this time, he called up the app, which controlled a network of five strategically positioned wireless security cameras with night vision. He selected the patio camera and was pleased to find no one displayed on his screen. Likewise, there was no message on his phone from the system telling him someone had entered their field of vision. Nor was there an automatically generated video, which occurred when someone was in camera range.

Yet Paul was still left with an uncomfortable feeling in the pit of his stomach. He was certain something had passed in front of that display. Perhaps it was a bird. Maybe a bird could have successfully flown under his patio roof and passed quickly in front of the screen. Paul realized the thing would have had to have been a bird of substantial size to block his view, even for a fraction of a second. In addition, a bird of that size might have triggered the motion-sensitive lights even though, to the best of Paul's recollections, no birds had ever done so previously. If so, he would also have to adjust the software parameters controlling the sensitivity of his cameras.

He continued to stare out at the glowing digital screen. After a few seconds, the screen once again went momentarily blank. It looked like whatever it was that had initially passed in front of the screen had done so again. However, this time, it moved from the right to the left. Looking down at his smartphone again, Paul hoped to see a notice appear from his camera software, telling him it detected motion and providing him with video, but there was nothing.

Paul grabbed a large butcher's knife from the knife block on the granite counter and slowly walked down the stairs to the two French doors leading out to his patio. If someone were out there, he would know momentarily, and if that person were looking for trouble, Paul would give him a healthy portion of it. He realized that what he was both thinking and doing was bluster. He had never even been in a single fight in his life and had no idea what he would do with the knife if someone confronted him. They'd probably disarm him and use his weapon against him. He was out of his league here, and the truth was, he was terrified.

He flipped on the patio light and cautiously opened the French door. Now, only a screen door separated him from the outside. He looked around the covered patio, then held the knife tightly in his right hand with the blade pointing downward. He opened the screen door and stepped out onto his veranda, hopefully, ready for whatever, if anything, awaited him outside. He looked around, but he saw no one, no intruder, no giant bird or bat. His phone beeped, alerting him that someone was standing on his patio. Paul looked down at his phone and saw himself standing alone in the doorway, looking ridiculous with a large knife in his hands.

Perhaps a gust of wind had blown something into his yard and across his line of sight, blocking the glow. But then Paul realized the wind would have had to shift and blow whatever it was back in the opposite direction. This seemed highly unlikely, especially since there appeared to be no wind. There wasn't even the slightest breeze. Paul looked over at the thermometer and saw the temperature had risen slightly to 30 degrees. It was still frigid for April, but the air was utterly still.

Besides, if something had blown across his patio, it likely would still be in his yard. On those occasions when things did blow into his backyard, they tended to stay there. A high privacy fence was on the eastern side of the yard, which he shared with his neighbor. When his neighbor had built his home on the empty lot next to Paul, he had the fence installed. Paul didn't mind as it saved him the expense of putting one up himself, at least along that side of his property. He had put a fence up along the remaining three sides of his yard, but that was a lower and much less expensive split rail fence with plastic-coated wire mesh attached. Paul had installed it himself to keep his dog from wandering.

Paul thought, *Good old Max*, his Golden Lab. Max had passed on more than two years ago. Paul wished he had Max now. Old Max would have been growling at the back door at the first sign of any strangeness in the yard and would have scared away any intruder. Being ninety-five pounds of growling dog with lots of sharp teeth had a way of doing that. The truth was, Max was as gentle as a kitten, probably more so, but one deep and loud "woof" from that gentle giant would make even the most self-assured bad guy rethink his plans.

Max was gone now, however, and it was just Paul alone who had to deal with this disturbing mystery. He carefully opened the patio door and stepped out into the cold morning air. He walked over to the left side of his patio, and as he stepped off onto the brick walkway, the motion-sensitive light did its job and showered that side of his property with light. No one was there. He walked to the right side of his patio and stepped off into the grass, wet with morning dew. The security light on that side of the house went on, and now the entire yard was awash with light.

Convinced that whatever he saw or whatever he thought he saw was nothing more than his imagination, Paul began to feel even more foolish standing there with a butcher's knife in his hand, like some psycho killer. He turned to go back into his house when he heard what sounded like a gentle voice whispering his name, "Paul."

He turned quickly, now brandishing his kitchen knife as if it were a longsword, no longer feeling foolish, confident he would find someone standing behind him. But there was no one. An icy chill raced down his spine, and despite the frigid temperatures, Paul could feel sweat forming at the center of his back and trickling downward. What was going on? Had he heard someone call his name, or was that too a product of his mind?

Paul went back inside the house, closed and locked the storm door, then closed and deadbolted the inside door. He left his patio light turned on. He'd turn it off later when he got home from work. He decided the small waste of electricity from the light burning all day was something he could accept for the peace of mind it would give him. He also decided he would leave the light on overnight as well, probably just for tonight. He realized he might be acting a bit weird about everything, but so be it.

When they were viewed in the light of day, he suspected that the strange feelings he had that morning would seem a bit ridiculous. Yet somewhere in the back of his mind, Paul still had an uncomfortable sensation. It was like a dimly lit bulb, barely noticeable but still able to cast enough light not to let him forget about how uneasy that morning's encounter had made him feel. Paul put all the strange feelings on the back burner throughout his busy workday and focused on doing his job. However, when the day was over, and he was driving home, he glanced at the setting sun in his rearview mirror and realized he wouldn't be home very long before the sun set entirely, and his backyard and patio would be thrown into darkness once again.

Why was he allowing the morning's few seconds of weirdness, no, perceived weirdness, to bother him again? The incident was nothing, a fluke, a glitch. Call it what you will, but it was a one-time occurrence that would likely never happen again. But what about that voice, the one that called his name? Was it only his overly stimulated imagination? Of course, it was. It had to be. It was most likely nothing more than a gentle breeze blowing through the pine trees. Yes, that had to be it.

When Paul arrived home, he pulled his car into the garage, closed the door, and carried his laptop bag up to the kitchen table. He always took the bag and the laptop computer inside to and from work daily. He glanced out his kitchen window and saw his patio still lit by the setting sun, but it wouldn't be long until that light was gone, and the patio would be thrust back into darkness. Then he remembered he had left the patio light on before going to work and felt better knowing that. As such, he went about his usual after-work routine and got ready for dinner. There wasn't much preparation to be done since he had stopped to pick up a pizza at his favorite local Italian take-out restaurant. It sat on his kitchen table in a box, still piping hot.

He went to the refrigerator, grabbed a cold beer, reached into a kitchen cabinet, and pulled out a dinner plate. He went over to his utensil drawer and pulled out a fork and steak knife. Paul didn't know anyone else who cut their pizza slice into bite-size pieces and ate it with a fork, but that was how he liked to do it. At least, that was how he did It until he got to the last few inches near the crust. Then, once he got there, he set down his fork and held the slice as everyone else did. Call him weird; he didn't care. He just hated to deal with that first segment of the pizza triangle, the one that dangled down like a limp noodle. Besides, He lived alone, and he ate alone, so he could do whatever he damn well pleased.

After he finished, he began wrapping the remainder of his pizza in plastic wrap. He put it in the refrigerator to munch on later in the week. He'd probably take a piece to work to nuke for lunch, although it was likely he'd end up munching on it cold at his desk long before lunch anyway. As he turned to close the refrigerator door, he noticed two things. First, it had gotten quite dark, much sooner than he had anticipated, and the overhead light on the patio was not lit.

Paul found this all perplexing. He knew he had left the light turned on because he checked and double-checked its status before leaving for work. Yet now, the light was off. Perhaps the bulb simply burned out. Paul knew that was unlikely since the light was part of an outdoor ceiling fan, which had a total of four bulbs. That meant that unless there was a problem with the fan unit or the electricity, all four of the bulbs had failed simultaneously.

He walked down to the family room and stood by the French doors leading to the patio. He slid up the switch that turned on the fan part of the unit and saw, not surprisingly, that the fan blades began to turn. So, there was power reaching the ceiling unit. He double-checked the switch and saw it was in the on position. Then, to be a bit obsessive/compulsive, he flicked the switch on and off several times to be sure. The lights didn't come on.

Paul grabbed a Maglite from a nearby cabinet and slowly opened the French door, stepping cautiously out onto the patio. He didn't exactly know why he was behaving the way he was. It was just a feeling, some primal understanding he had that told him to be careful and, if necessary, be afraid. The sun hadn't set yet, so it wasn't dark out on the patio. He hadn't needed to use his Maglite yet. He was sure if he stepped off either side of the patio, neither motion light would activate. He got an alert on his cellphone and looked down at his screen, seeing himself standing outside on the patio alone.

He stood in the semi-darkness, waiting. He was expecting some indicator of what was happening and what he should do about it. Perhaps he was allowing his imagination to get the best of him. After all, all the lights might have burned out at the same time. A spike of electric current could do that. It was also possible there was a problem with the ceiling fan itself. It was more than fifteen years old and had been out here all that time. Sure, the patio was covered, but the fan was still exposed to extreme heat and cold. Plus, there was humidity and dryness to consider. The more Paul thought about it, the more sense that scenario made. He turned and looked back at the time and temperature unit mounted on a pole about ten feet away.

As he looked, a dark shadow flew in front of the digital screen as it had done early that morning. Yet Paul heard nothing, not the flapping of wings or the fluttering of material. There was no sound, and there had been no one there. But what had passed between him and the device? He began to slowly back up toward the French door as the hair on the back of his neck stood on end, and a cold chill ran down his spine. Then, impossibly, he heard something. It came in a faint whisper like a breeze blowing through tall grass. It was the same thing he had heard that morning. He heard a faint whispering, almost hissing voice call his name.

"Paul . . . Paul. We are calling you Paul," the voice said.

"Who . . . Who is that?"

There was no reply. Paul suddenly realized someone from his job might be screwing with him. Several of his coworkers were known for being pranksters and practical jokers. One or more of them might have gotten together and decided. It was time for a "mess with Paul" event. That seemed to make more sense than any alternative scenario, especially ones dealing with unseen creatures calling to him from the shadows.

"Nice. Nice. I get it now," Paul called to the darkness, "somebody's out there with a microphone and a night vision camera screwing with me and filming the whole thing. Is that you, Benny? Or is it Jonesy? Hell, maybe it's both of you morons working together. Maybe between the two of you, you were able to come up with half a brain."

But there was no reply, not a sound. That was when Paul noticed for the first time that there wasn't a single bird chirping, not a solitary cricket sound to be heard. The night was as quiet as . . . as a grave. That thought sent chills racing down Paul's spine. That was when he heard the whispering voice again.

"Don't be frightened, Paul. We are here for you," the voice said.

"Who are you? What are you? Why can't I see you?" Paul asked in a trembling voice.

"You can't see us because we can't be seen yet."

Paul said, "You keep saying 'we.' How many of you are there?"

There was a brief hesitation, then the voice said, "We are as many as we need to be. We are the children of the night. We come and go. We ebb and flow. We are here for you. If you want us to."

Paul asked, confused, "What is that? Some sort of poem? Children of the night, my left butt cheek. I don't know what is happening here, but I'm going back inside where none of this insanity exists."

"We can make all of your fantasies a reality, Paul. We can give you everything you've ever dreamed of and more."

Paul stopped in his tracks. He might not want to believe all this hocus pocus, mumbo jumbo crap, but one thing he did know about was making a deal.

He asked, "But if that's true, I have to ask, why me? What's so special about me that you so-called 'children of the night' feel the need to help me?"

There was a slight hesitation, then the voice said, "You are correct, Paul. You are not special. But you are you, and that makes you unique."

"If that's the case, then everyone in the world is unique in their way, so again, I ask why me."

"Because you're here. And here is where we are. So here is now, and now is here, and we are here with you and here for you."

Paul said, "What if I don't want your help? What if I don't want whatever it is you're offering?"

"Then we will move on. We will leave you forever. We will be elsewhere with someone else and will make that person the same offer we have made to you."

"But why do you do this? What's the meaning? What's the purpose?"

"We are who we are, and we must do what we must do. We are children of the night, and we do what we need to do."

Paul thought about it for a few moments. It was all starting to sound too good to be true. Whoever these creatures, these night children were, that seemed to be offering him a pretty sweet deal. He thought about his life as it currently was and was not impressed. He was divorced with a huge mortgage. He had to buy his ex-wife out of the house as part of the settlement. They had no kids, but he still got nailed for alimony payments every week. He had a dead-end job he hated, which had no chance for advancement. His boss was an arrogant, overpaid moron who Paul fantasized about killing in many different and creative ways. Financially, his life was in the crapper, and sexually, it was even worse. He hadn't had a date in more than a year. He figured he had nothing to lose. Maybe he should give these clowns a try.

"So, what do I have to do to accept your help?"

"It is quite easy. Simply invite us into your home. Once you do, you will be able to see us, and we can give you everything you deserve."

Something about all this didn't feel right. There was some little thought bouncing around in the back of his mind, something he thought he should know, but for the life of him, he couldn't remember. Maybe he should forget all this. He did not doubt that whatever these creatures might be, the odds of them being able to do what they were promising was slim to none. But what if they could?

Then, before he even fully realized what he was doing, Paul held open the patio door and said, "Children of the night. Please come inside. You are all most welcome here. Mi casa, es su casa, and all that nonsense."

As Paul stood holding the door, he felt something pass by him. He suddenly realized it was several somethings entering his house. He saw nothing but sensed them as they went by. His family room had a hardwood floor, but Paul suspected if it was carpeted, he might have seen either footprints or at least a rustling of the carpet fibers as they passed. If he were to guess, he would have said he had sensed two or three of them go by and could now feel their presence in his family room. He stepped inside and pulled the door closed behind him. As he did, the creatures began to take shape before him. The transformation taking place reminded Paul of when he was a boy, and he would lie on his living room floor for hours watching the dust particles floating in rays of sunlight. However, the glowing particles He was now seeing were swirling in circular patterns in the air, coming together and solidifying into . . . well, into people, he supposed.

Perhaps the term people was too generous a word to use. In this instance . . . beings might be more accurate. As he had sensed, there were three of "them," whatever "them" constituted, standing directly across the room from him in front of his large flat-screen TV. The first creature he noticed appeared to be male. He was short and round, perhaps four feet tall and equal in circumference. The little man had shoulder-length grey hair and a long white beard that grew from under a bushy mustache and traveled down past the middle of his chest. His clothing was nothing special, just jeans, a flannel shirt, and sneakers, all of which were well-worn. The creature wore a tall, pointed hat, and Paul would have easily mistaken him for an oversized yard gnome. His cherubic round face wore a big closed-mouth smile.

In the center was a cute, red-haired, pixie-like little female standing about five feet tall, with short hair, slightly pointed ears, huge blue eyes, and voluptuous red lips. She was wearing a tight-fitting black leotard, which was simultaneously low-cut on top, revealing plenty of cleavage and high-cut on the bottom, leaving very little to the imagination in that area as well. She offered Paul a smile that was miles beyond alluring. That look radiated sensuality so intense that Paul felt he might die if he didn't find a way to break free of her siren's spell. She was the most beautiful creature Paul had ever seen, and he realized he would trade all the promises these creatures made for just night with this vixen.

When he finally freed his gaze from the woman, he saw the third creature. Paul was unsure if that being was male or female. It appeared to be a young boy but could easily be a girl. There was nothing about this androgynous youth that could be considered sexual in any way. This being stared at Paul with its mysterious Mona Lisa-like smile. Paul found this creature to be the most disturbing of the three strangers.

"I suppose I wasn't sure what you would look like," Paul admitted.

Although none of the three opened their mouths or appeared to speak a word, Paul heard them all simultaneously inside his mind, saying, "We appear as you want us to appear."

Paul pointed to the first creature and said, "Are you saying I wanted you to look like a giant garden gnome, so that's how you appeared to me?"

"Yes," the three voices said in his mind.

"OK, I suppose I understand that. I've seen plenty of garden gnomes in my day, but you other two . . . where did your images come from."

"We are from you. We are here for you."

That cryptic declaration did nothing to help relieve Paul's confusion. "You mean to say if I decided to change the way you all look, I could do that?"

The three creatures began to change again before the words had left his lips. Their forms disappeared into a swirling mass of glowing particles, only to reform into three new, surprisingly different, and much more satisfying shapes. All three were now women, and not just women, but three beautiful and entirely naked women.

"OK then. That's more like it," Paul said.

The three women stood silently in Paul's family room, the curves of their backs traveling down to their naked backsides, reflecting on the blank screen of the giant television behind them.

Paul found himself getting quite aroused by the images before him. He asked, "So now what? When will you give me everything I deserve in life, as you promised? I mean, I can suddenly think of several things you can do for me right this very minute."

The three women walked toward Paul and began stroking his face and hair. Then they slowly unbuttoned his shirt and peeled it off of him as they rubbed themselves against his naked chest and back. Paul had fantasized about encounters like this many times in his life.

The three voices said in his mind, "Is this what you want, Paul? Is this your wildest fantasy? Is this something you've always dreamed of?"

Paul was going out of his mind with ecstasy, repeatedly moaning, "Yes, yes, oh yes. Don't stop. I want more."

That was when he felt the first bite tearing into his throat.

"Whaaaaglglg!" Paul cried with a gurgling moan.

"You were right to wonder why we chose you, Paul. We chose you because we knew how desperate you were. Also, we knew how gullible and greedy you were. You were desperate, gullible, and stupid enough to believe our lies. We said we were here for you, Paul, and we are here for you, but not in the way you might think. We are not here to help you. We are here to consume you."

Paul screamed again as he felt a chunk of his right arm torn off. He tried to fight off his attackers, but they were too strong. He heard their voices again in his head.

You were so stupid and so wrong to invite us into your home. Had you not done so, we couldn't have hurt you. Paul recalled how he had almost not asked these creatures in. Then he felt his left arm ripped from its socket and saw the blood squirting like a fountain from the tattered flesh stump. His vision began to fade to black, and Paul knew soon his pain would be gone.

As the last of his life left his body, he felt the agony of his stomach being torn out, and he heard his innards falling to the hardwood floor with a disgusting splattering plop and the chewing sounds of the children of the night.

REJECTION

"We all learn lessons in life. Some stick, some don't.
I have always learned more from rejection and failure
than from acceptance and success."
—HENRY ROLLINS

"I really wish I was less of a thinking man and more
of a fool not afraid of rejection."
—BILLY JOEL

"Sometimes I feel my whole life has been one big rejection."
—MARILYN MONROE

"Most fears of rejection rest on the desire for approval from other
people. Don't base your self-esteem on their opinions."
—HARVEY MACKAY

Becky's eyes fluttered open as she slowly crawled her way out of the
darkness back to the world of consciousness. She woke with her head
hanging down, her chin on her chest and a steady stream of rapidly
cooling drool dripping off her chin. As her vision cleared, she could see
her legs, her naked legs, but couldn't seem to grasp the significance of
what she was seeing.

The room around her was dark, save for a few candles burning
on a nearby dresser. It was one of those tall five-drawer dressers her

grandmother used to call a . . . What was it? A big boy? No, it was a high boy. Although the flickering light was minimal, it was bright enough for Becky to recognize the dresser had seen better days. It was scared and faded, and its remaining paint was chipping and peeling. The wood was split in places, and one of the drawers hung askew.

The soles of her feet were cold as if they were resting against a concrete floor. Likewise, the air around her was cool and damp. She was sure she was in a basement. Across the room, thick curtains were hanging over a tiny window high up near the open-beamed ceiling. The window was visible only as a sliver where the curtains met. She could tell it was almost sunset outside. Once again, she noticed the room's dank, musty odor much more strongly, now realizing it was the stench of decay. There was also the faint aroma of the melting candle wax and a sulfur-tinged burning that made her wonder strangely for a moment why the candles weren't scented. That certainly would have improved things. She realized that was an odd thought for her to have in such a confusing situation.

Becky found she was unable to focus. She felt peculiar, as if she were coming down from some anesthetic. Dreamlike surrealism seemed to engulf her. Then she noticed discomfort in her back and realized something was wrong. She seemed to be sitting upright in a wooden chair of some sort. As she edged closer to consciousness, she was able to sense her flesh pressing against the chair's hard, smooth, and cold wooden surface.

When she tried to lift her arms, Becky looked down and saw they both had been duct-taped to the arms of the heavy chair. As she tried to move her feet, she felt her ankles were likewise bound to the chair. Panicking, Becky tried to rock the chair first front-to-back, then left-to-right, but her attempts were useless. It became apparent that in addition to the chair being heavy, it was fastened somehow securely to the floor. Perhaps it was cemented or bolted in place. Whatever the case, the thing wouldn't budge.

Now completely awake, Becky did a quick inventory of herself to see just what sort of trouble she had. With relief, she saw she was not completely naked and still wore her bra and panties. However, the relief was short-lived. Someone had brought her to this place—wherever this place was and had removed her clothing and secured her in this chair. But for what reason, and perhaps more importantly, to what eventual purpose? Becky decided her best chance was to go on the offensive and do her best not to show the fear she felt inside.

She shouted into the darkness, "What the Hell is this? Who are you? I demand to know what this is all about!"

A chair scraped somewhere in a shadowed corner of the room as its inhabitant stood and slowly came into view. In his late twenties, he was a gaunt young man with long, dark, greasy black hair and more tattoos and piercings than she had ever seen on one person before. He wore a filthy, yellowed wife-beater tee shirt and equally dirty and faded jeans. Strangely, his feet were clad in a new, clean pair of florescent pink Crocs. He stared at Becky through dark, haunted raccoon eyes as his mouth hung agape in a hang-dog expression. There was a rank, unwashed odor about him, and when he spoke, his breath was as foul as a sewer.

"Hello, Becky. I've been waiting for you to wake up. You reacted poorly to the drug I used to bring you here. For a while, I thought you might be dead. That would have been bad." He smiled what would have been a big, toothy grin had it not been for his twisted collection of brown and rotten teeth looking like broken tombstones in an ancient cemetery.

As Becky stared at the man's soiled, filthy and unshaven face, she saw something crawling from the frayed top of his tee-shirt and up along his neck. It was a tiny spider. She loathed spiders. It didn't matter how small or unthreatening the thing might be; she was terrified of all spiders. She couldn't recall the origin of her arachnophobia but suspected it must have formed at a very early age because, for as long as she could remember, it had been her greatest of fears.

The young man lifted his hand, plucked the spider from his grime-covered neck, and stared closely at it for a few seconds. For a moment, Becky was sure the man would either crush the spider in his fingers or put the wriggling thing into his mouth and eat it alive. Because that was the sort of thing crazy people did, and it was apparent that this wretched creature standing before her was as insane as someone could be. To make matters worse, She was his helpless prisoner. Then he slowly held the spider out to her, putting the twitching arachnid an inch from her face. It took everything Becky had not to scream in terror as its legs wiggled in front of her.

Her captor said in a calm and disturbingly normal voice, "I've done my research as all good authors should and learned that you have a terrible fear of spiders, Becky. Is that true? I was amazed to learn it because here you are, running a successful publishing company, yet you're terrified of these tiny creatures. This is the same woman who decides daily, whose stories are good enough to publish, and who gets rejected. I mean, seriously, Becky, you could crush one of these tiny creatures in your hands as easily as you crush the dreams and spirits of young writers hoping for a break."

With that, the young man did crush the spider between his dirty fingers. When he did, liquid shot forward and splattered Becky's creek. Struggling to turn her face away from both the remains of the spider as well as the man's rank breath, Becky managed to demand, "Who are you? How do you know me? Why am I here?"

"Questions, questions. So many questions. You truly are the curious sort, aren't you, Becky, my dear," the man said as he flicked the crushed spider off his fingers and onto Becky's leg.

"Oh please, no. Jesus no. Please take it off me," Becky cried in terror as all the bravado she had managed to muster vanished.

"Relax, relax," the man said as he flicked the spider carcass with his finger, sending it flying across the room into the shadows.

Becky stared down at her leg as every muscle in her body tensed, "Please, please get that too."

The man looked a bit confused until he noticed one of the spider's legs still lying on Becky's naked thigh.

"Ok, ok, I'll get it. Wow! You certainly do have some serious issues with our little spider-friends, don't you?" He picked off the leg, held it between his fingers, which still bore the residual goo from the crushed spider, and brushed it gently across Becky's clenched and trembling lips.

Her terror came out as a high-pitched keening emanating from her nose and throat, sounding like whimpering on a wounded kitten. Her eyes were held tightly shut as tears streamed down her cheeks. When, at last, she no longer felt the leg brushing her lips, and she heard the sound of her captor stepping away, she unclenched her lips and opened her eyes. The young man was standing a few feet in front of her, grinning his rotten-toothed grin.

"God, how I enjoyed that!"

Becky was on the verge of hysteria. She pleaded, "Why . . . why are you . . . are you doing this to me? I don't know . . . who you are. Please . . . Please . . ."

"That's right, Becky, my dear. You don't know who I am. And thanks to you and people like you, no one knows who I am. But you don't care about that, do you? For you, it's just another day at the office, running your horror publishing business. You're the queen at Terror Tales Publishing, aren't you? You're the Lord High Muckity-muck of your industry. You read a submission, wave your magic wand or royal scepter and decide yea or nay. Isn't that right, Becky? To you, it's all just words on a page, subject to whatever mood you happen to be in on any particular day. You never take the time to think about what effect your rejection might have on a struggling author like me."

"You . . . you're an author?" She asked, struggling desperately to try to make some sense out of something so senseless.

"Oh yes, I most certainly am. And apparently, I seem to be one of your favorite targets for rejection."

"Look, I'm sorry . . . but I'm afraid I don't know you or what I've done to upset you."

"Horror in Paradise," the man said.

Becky was confused, "What? I don't understand."

The man was becoming agitated and started rattling off what at first Becky thought were unrelated phrases, getting louder and angrier with each utterance, "Horror In Paradise! I Eat Your Young! Death At Daycare! Incestual Terror!"

That last one especially triggered a faint memory. Incestual Terror? What was that? Then, it all started to come into focus. All those phrases were short story titles. She had heard them all before. Hell, she had read and rejected them all. Then, a name popped into her mind.

She looked at the young man and whispered knowingly, "Artimus Dread?"

"Ah, yes. So, you do remember," he replied.

Becky remembered very well the pseudonym—she was sure it was a pseudonym—Artimus Dread was an author who had submitted dozens of short stories to her publishing company. And she had rejected every one of them, and for good reasons. Not only was the writing amateurish at best, the grammar ridiculous, and the spelling atrocious, but the moron never once even attempted to follow her submission guidelines. As if that weren't bad enough, the subject matter of his stories was not only in violation of her publishing company policy but went against even the lowest of moral codes, as the story titles alone suggested.

When she received the first story, "Horror In Paradise," she was curious even though it is evident from the first sentence that the story would be garbage. She could still recall that first line of the story. It seemed to haunt her like a hated tune that got stuck in her head.

She recalled the ridiculous opening line, "Although they were stranded on a beautiful island paradise, their sexual and cannibalistic urges would soon turn it into a Hell on earth."

Becky looked at her captor and said, "You."

"Yes, me, Becky. How many of my stories did you reject? A dozen? Two dozen? Maybe more. In the beginning, you would simply send a generic email reply saying something like, 'We're sorry, but we have to pass on this at this time. Good luck placing it elsewhere.' But eventually, that wasn't enough, was it? After a while, you had to start adding your editorial comments to my rejections, comments like 'juvenile, sophomoric, embarrassing' to name a few. And as if that weren't bad enough, you had to step up your game with words like 'sick, twisted and warped.' Nice move, Becky, real nice."

"Look . . . I'm . . . I'm sorry . . ."

"Shut up, you insolent ignorant bitch! I'm the one in charge now! I'm the new Lord High Muckity-muck! I'm the editor in this story!" He screamed at the top of his lungs.

He stood in front of her, panting like a dog for a few moments, trying desperately to regain his composure. He had a plan for this woman, and he couldn't allow his anger to cause him to do something to change that plan. True, she would end up dead either way, but the plan was a much more suitable path to follow.

He released a deep, stinking breath and said calmly, "I especially recall the last rejection email you sent. That one was for 'Incestual Terror.' You said, and I quote, 'You are one of the sickest bastards I have ever encountered. You should quit writing, crawl back into whatever primordial sludge you crawled out of, and do us all a favor by curling up and dying.' Becky, oh my sweet Becky. That was not very nice of you now, was it? You, of all people, should know to stick to the standard, polite and generic rejection letter format. A publisher should never offer such a blatant criticism of an author's work. If so, such a publisher might find herself in a situation she can't handle, like this one."

"What . . . what do you want from me?" Becky pleaded.

The young man smiled his hideous grin and said, "Want? What do I want? Why, Becky, I thought someone as smart as you claim to be would have already figured that out by now. I want you to die. And I want you to die slowly, painfully and to lose your mind before death finally comes to claim you."

"No . . . please . . . I'm sorry. I truly am. Look, I'll make a deal with you. Let me go . . . and I promise I'll publish your stories. I'll even do an entire book of your work. You . . . you won't have to share the pages with anyone. It will be all yours."

"Too much, too little, too late, as the song goes, Becky. There's no need for you to compromise your precious literary integrity. I'm already in the process of self-publishing on one of the many websites available, so, as you can see, I am no longer in need of your services."

Becky said, "But what about promotion? I . . . I could help promote your work if you did it through our company."

"Sorry, Sweetie. That ship has sailed for you, I'm afraid. Now, give me a second or two to get ready, then I'll be saying goodbye . . . forever."

Becky watched in terror as the young man walked over to one end of the room and pulled out a video camera on a tripod. He must have stolen it somewhere because it was apparent he could never have afforded such a camera. He pointed the lens at her, and she could see him focusing on getting the right image.

He said, "I could use my cell phone for this, but to do so, I would have to stay here in the room with you, and that wouldn't be good for me. The special treat I have in store for you is not something I wouldn't want to be part of for my health and well-being. I'll return eventually when I render this room safe again, that is after you're dead."

"What . . . what are you going to do to me?"

"Oh, you'll see very soon, sweet Becky."

The man walked to the shadowy area to the right of the tripod and slid a two-foot square wooden crate over into the light. He looked at Becky and gave that decayed jack-o-lantern grin one last time. He pulled off the lid of the trunk and quickly backed away into the shadows. Becky heard the slamming of a door and knew her captor was gone. She was alone . . . with whatever was inside the box.

She stared at the black opening of the crate, waiting with dreadful anticipation of what might be inside. She believed she knew but hoped against all hope that she was wrong. She was not wrong. Within a few seconds, she saw something hook itself over the top of the box. It was thin, black, and hairy. She immediately recognized it as a leg . . . a huge spider's leg. Soon, other legs made their way out of the box, followed by the furry bodies of several other giant arachnids.

Then the smaller ones came, skittering over the backs of the larger ones. Then the jumpers came next; horrid little things jumped down to the floor with ease. There were dozens of the wretched creatures, no hundreds. Like a flood of legs and fur-covered bodies, the spiders kept coming. Becky's breath caught in her throat. She wanted to scream, had to scream, but couldn't find the air to do so. She realized with horror that there were thousands of spiders. Most of them scurried to the darker, shadowed areas of the room, but far too many crawled toward her.

When she felt the first spider creeping onto her foot, Becky was uncertain whether it had been real or if perhaps her fear-stimulated brain had imagined the sensation. As terror raced through her with the speed of a bullet, Becky decided not to look down. If she didn't see the creature, maybe she could convince herself these phantom sensations were nothingness than her vivid imagination working overtime. She had just about convinced herself when she felt a second one, then a third. Soon, her feet and ankles were awash with the feeling of hundreds of tiny legs crawling about her feet and working their way up her ankles.

Reluctantly, Becky opened her eyes just as several spiders made their way over her knees and up onto her thighs. She shook her legs as best as she was able, screaming, crying, and thrashing, trying her best to shake the horrible things off her legs. That was when she felt the first stinging bite, which sent a red-hot flame into the meat of her thigh. Then she felt another and another. Too late, she realized her thrashing had done nothing but agitate the creatures and cause them to attack her.

As she sat trembling, too terrified to try to shake them off any longer, the spiders continued to crawl up past her thighs and onto her bare stomach. She could feel the hundreds of tiny insectile feet scurrying up her belly and onto her breasts. Becky began to feel strange. Her legs had become numb, and her thoughts were becoming confused as if she were falling asleep. She felt several additional hot stings on her stomach and upper chest.

Becky had stopped crying. She had stopped panicking. As if accepting her fate, or perhaps it was the result of the quantities of spider venom in her system, she calmly sat as the spiders did their work. Maybe it wasn't the toxins that had caused this. Perhaps her captor was right, and she had lost her sanity. She supposed that was a possibility since no sane person could sit still while hundreds of spiders covered her body and continued to sting and bite her repeatedly.

Now, they were crawling up her neck and over her chin, trying desperately to get between her tightly clenched lips. Several smaller spiders crawled up into her nostrils. Becky sneezed involuntarily, her body reacting to the tickling sensation inside her nose. But soon enough, creatures had blocked her nostrils, and she was no longer able to breathe. She knew what would happen if she allowed her mouth to open, but she had no choice. She opened wide and took what would be her last cleansing breath and could feel hundreds of tiny, shuffling feet crawl over her lips, filling her mouth and slithering down her throat. She knew this was the end. Her last thought iconically was that some people don't handle rejection very well.

-

www.ingramcontent.com/pod-product-compliance
Lightning Source LLC
Chambersburg PA
CBHW020331260626
47156CB00004B/1480